Beyond the
Black Mist

A Familiar Curse Story by
C.L. Bright

Also by C.L. Bright

The Spellcaster's Trap
Sins of the Shadow Walkers

Acknowledgments

I want to thank everyone who helped me with this new series. I really appreciate my daughters for inspiring me to take a chance with this genre. They have been asking me to write books they can read for the last couple of years. I also want to thank Levenia for being my sounding board as I built this new world. My beta readers, April, Kari, and Yvonne, are amazing and really helped me work out the final bugs in these books.

Thank you to my fabulous cover designer, J.N. Sheats, who is also an amazing author. Finally, thank you Kendra for catching my typos.

Chapter One

Dante

At least Juliet and Serena had gotten away.

I kept reminding myself of that as I laid on the cot in my prison cell. Around my ankle was a cuff with a spell to strip me of all magic. I'd never been without magic before.

The spell left me feeling weak. At first, I'd also had trouble focusing on anything, though that could have been due to the head injury I'd sustained during my capture.

With no windows, it was hard to say exactly how long I'd been locked up, but I suspected I'd been there five days. The lights inside the room remained at the same level day and night, so I was basing my guess on how much my wounds from the fight had healed.

My cell was one of three in this particular section of the detention area and the only one occupied. Outside of the cells was a small area for visitors.

I caught only glimpses of dim artificial lighting when someone entered from the outside corridor, leading me to believe I was in one of the belowground levels reserved for high-risk prisoners.

Shifting slightly, I cringed. I had plenty of new injuries, thanks to Nicolas. He wanted to make sure I suffered every day. Torturing any prisoner violated Azurean laws, but I hadn't bothered complaining to the guards. After having lied about Juliet, my word was worth very little. I also suspected a lot of spellcasters didn't care if my brother added to my punishment since they considered me a traitor.

I was well and truly screwed, but I didn't regret my actions. Serena and Juliet would have fared far worse had Nicolas gotten his hands on either of them. I'd seen the way he'd looked at Juliet. He'd have hurt her and used her.

Nicolas had stayed away so far that day, but I suspected he'd be back to gloat after my hearing. The hearing would determine my punishment. My guilt wasn't in question. All that remained was to determine the severity of my crimes.

Closing my eyes, I pictured Juliet as she'd been in her larger cat form. There was no question she'd used some of my power to take on her new form. I'd never experienced or seen anything like that before.

All my life, I'd been told a familiar could enhance a spellcaster's magic. The spellcaster gave nothing in return, yet that's not how my bond with Juliet worked. Some of Juliet's power had entered me, but it had felt more like an even exchange that bound us together.

Somehow, our magic was woven together in a knot that I could easily visualize. I saw where the pieces connected me to Juliet. I'd lost my telepathic link to her—a fact that made me feel empty inside. My inability to touch her mind could be due to the dampening spell or the distance between us. The connection might have been temporary. I felt lost without it.

"Dante? Are you awake?"

My eyes opened, and I struggled to my feet at the sound of Laranissa's voice.

"Hey." It was all I could think to say to the only mother I'd ever known.

Since my arrest, I'd cared very little about what anyone thought of me. Only Nicolas had visited. Though it hurt, I wasn't surprised by my father's rejection. I'd been almost relieved when Ambrose and Laranissa hadn't come. I didn't want to see the accusation in their eyes.

Laranissa's eyes narrowed as she looked at me. "Who did this to you?"

One corner of my lips kicked up. "You're angry because I was injured during my apprehension?"

"I'm angry because something tells me part of this damage happened after you were apprehended," she stated. "These bruises are new. Am I right?"

I shrugged and winced at the pain in my shoulder. "It doesn't matter."

She started to argue before shaking her head and taking a deep breath. "Why did you bring Juliet back here? They said you knew she was a shapeshifter when you brought her here. Why would you put yourself at risk like that?"

It struck me as odd that she referred to Juliet as a *shapeshifter* rather than a *familiar*.

"I found her in a trap, fully-clothed and in human form. I thought she was a witch."

She nodded her understanding. "It makes sense that you assumed she was a witch at first, but you knew the truth before you brought her here."

"I found out when I kissed her. The reaction between our magic was strange and intense. I've never felt anything like it. Juliet fascinated me, and when she told me she was from the Heathergate Refuge, I believed her. Juliet's stepmother wanted her out of the way so her son could become the next leader. She stole Juliet's bracelet and left her in a trap."

I sighed when I saw the doubt in her expression. "I know it sounds crazy, but that's what happened."

"If Juliet's stepmother wanted her out of the way, then why not kill her?"

"Likely for the same reason Nicolas didn't kill me. Her stepmother sounds like the type who would want to inflict the most suffering. Having Juliet forced into slavery must have seemed crueler than death."

I could pretend my brother hadn't killed me because he loved me, but I wasn't an idiot. Laranissa didn't argue.

"And you're sure she's not a rebel?" she asked. "I don't think you can count on her clothing to prove she's telling the truth."

"She's telling the truth," I insisted.

"You have so much faith in her," Laranissa whispered.

"I would trust her with my life," I replied.

"You did," she reminded me. "She left you to deal with Nicolas alone."

"It's not that simple," I argued. "She only left after I told her to get Serena to safety. When Nicolas attacked with the other spellcasters, Juliet and the shapeshifter with us could have made a run for it. Thanks to Juliet and the other shapeshifter, Serena is safe."

"I hope you're right about Serena being safe," Laranissa remarked. "The hatred between our kind and theirs runs deep on both sides. It's largely rooted in ignorance. Each side has their version of what happened, but not many know the truth."

"Are you claiming to know the truth?" I asked. This was a side of Laranissa I'd never seen. She'd always avoided topics that could be considered the least bit controversial.

"That's a talk for another time," she told me. "For now, we need to find a way to get you out of this mess. Your father won't help you because he believes your brother's lies. Nicolas is telling everyone who'll listen that you've known Juliet for months and that you're a traitor who's chosen to align himself with the rebels. According to him, you and Juliet were planning a rebel shapeshifter attack on Azuredale."

I blew out a frustrated breath. "That explains why I'm still locked up. My crimes are serious, but I expected to be confined to our home until the hearing. At most, I thought I'd get house arrest after the hearing, but that's not likely if the justice panel believes Nicolas. This is much worse than

I imagined."

"Are you regretting helping Juliet yet?" she asked, watching me with a strange intensity.

I shook my head, not needing to consider my answer. "I'll take whatever punishment they hand down if it means Juliet and Serena are free."

Laranissa nodded. "I was hoping you'd say that."

"You're acting very out of character," I accused.

"One of my boys is in serious trouble," she replied. "I love you, Dante."

"I love you, too," I whispered. "You have no idea how much your support means to me. You've always been a mother to me, and I'm not sure I could handle losing your love."

"That will never happen. I'm going to get you out of here," she promised.

"It's okay if you can't," I assured her. "Don't risk yourself for me. Nicolas will find a way to make you pay for it later."

"So, you think I should ignore the danger you're in?"

"I think you should avoid putting yourself in danger to help me. When I decided to help Juliet, I knew I'd be punished if I got caught."

She smiled and met my gaze. "Helping you is far from the riskiest thing I've ever done. Don't worry about me. I know how to avoid getting caught a lot better than you."

I had no clue how to take those strange words, and she didn't give me a chance to ask for an explanation before she hurried out of the room.

Chapter Two

My hearing was delayed, and during my wait, Nicolas came by several times to interrogate me. Twice, he brought others with him to question me. Those times, he'd focused on trying to get me to tell him where he could find Serena. I wasn't lying about not knowing where she was, but he was right to assume I wouldn't tell him if I did know.

When Nicolas came on his own, I got a frightening glimpse of the madness he kept hidden from others. I felt certain he'd have helped me escape if I offered to lead him to Juliet. His obsession with her terrified me, and I took comfort in knowing that he had no clue where to find her.

Search parties had scoured the area where we'd met up with Alaric, but they'd found no traces of a settlement. Nicolas told me that in a rage-filled rant where he swore he'd have Juliet. That would happen over my dead body.

I had begun to wonder if Nicolas planned to beat me to death before my hearing when I was finally summoned.

By the time I walked toward the defendant's table in cuffs, I was certain I had a few broken ribs, and my right shoulder had been dislocated. Though I'd managed to get my shoulder back into the socket, it still throbbed with my hands cuffed behind my back.

Based on the glares from those in attendance,

everyone already believed the stories of my links to the rebels and hoped for a harsh punishment.

"Come and stand up here," one of the judges commanded.

The five judges who would decide my fate sat at the front of the room, each in crimson robes. The justice panel consisted of three witches and two warlocks: Hattie Frost, Davina Stone, Lucia Brevil, Wade Denholm, and Jameson Drake. They'd been fair and listened to Serena's side at her hearing, even going so far as to censure those who called her a traitor.

Not one looked at me with an ounce of sympathy, so I doubted I'd get the same treatment.

"Dante Verdugo," Hattie Frost began in a grave tone. "You stand accused of conspiring with our enemies and plotting a rebellion. You are also accused of attempted murder and aiding in the escape of Serena Verdugo, who is accused of attempted murder. Do you have anything to say for yourself?"

"Yes, but I would like to first speak on behalf of my cousin, Serena Verdugo."

"She'll speak for herself when she's captured!" Nicolas shouted.

"If you can't remain silent, Nicolas Verdugo, you will be removed," Jameson Drake warned. "Am I making myself clear?"

I caught Nicolas's look of fury out of the corner of my eye and enjoyed the way he struggled to get his temper under control.

"Of course," Nicolas replied with barely suppressed rage. "Forgive my interruption. I'm still having trouble accepting this betrayal from members of my family. My baby brother tried to kill me."

"I understand," Hattie told him, though she still sounded annoyed with his interruption. "Regardless of your emotional state, you will not turn this into a theatrical event." Her attention shifted to me. "What is it you want to say regarding Serena Verdugo?"

"Serena didn't try to kill anyone," I stated.

"What would you call throwing a knife at someone?" she asked.

"She could have easily hit that warlock in the heart. My cousin didn't want to kill anyone," I insisted. "She's also not a traitor."

"Her actions say otherwise," Hattie replied.

"I know it looks bad, but Serena wanted to help Juliet," I insisted. "Juliet saved my life, and Serena felt she owed her."

"There are some who claim the nāga attack was arranged to make your familiar look like a hero so she could gain the trust of others in Azuredale," Lucia Brevil remarked.

"I'm not stupid enough to get bitten by a nāga to prove Juliet can be trusted. Even if *you* don't believe Juliet saved my life, Serena believes she did."

The panel all gave slight nods, and Hattie said, "We'll take what you've said into consideration when we sentence Serena. Now, back to you. Why were you in that area the day of your alleged attack? Is it close to the rogue familiar settlement?"

"I don't know if it's near their settlement," I replied. "It may be, but I've never been there."

"I find that hard to believe since you knew where to meet one of the rebels," Hattie scoffed. "Why would a rebel come out to meet you if you weren't already working with them?"

"I saved his life, and he told Juliet that she could go to the area where we dropped him off if she ever needed help. How he found us, I'm not sure."

"So, this rebel was a friend of the familiar you brought to Azuredale." Hattie didn't give me a chance to respond. "You admit to bringing a rebel here and pretending she was a witch to conceal her presence from others."

"She's not a rebel." I let out a sigh. "You won't believe me no matter what I say."

"Try me," she coaxed.

"Juliet really isn't a rebel," I insisted.

"Then what is she?" she demanded.

"She's the next in line to lead the Heathergate Refuge," I replied.

"And she just happened to be wandering around with no way to prove her identity?" Jameson asked. "Not only that, she had no bracelet."

"I know it sounds crazy," I agreed. "So does a rebel running around fully clothed. That's how I found her in a trap."

"That would be strange if it's true." Hattie didn't need to say more. There was no reason for them to believe a word I'd said. "Your brother, Nicolas, told us you were going to claim the familiar was from the Heathergate Refuge. We sent messages asking if they had any missing members. All are accounted for. If the next in line to lead were missing, they would have told us."

She could be lying to get me to confess. If she'd gotten the same information as Torrent, she'd have heard that Juliet had been killed while away from the Heathergate Refuge for the first time. That would give some credibility to my story.

The messenger she'd sent might have spoken to someone in on Juliet's death. If they'd only asked about missing members, Juliet's name might not have come up since they believed she was dead.

I couldn't tell them what Torrent had heard since I didn't want to get him into trouble. He was my best witness, but I suspected he'd be locked up with me if anyone heard that he'd been willing to help Juliet.

How could I possibly convince them of the truth to lessen my sentence?

I could think of no way to prove my innocence.

"Disappointed that we already checked on your lie?" Hattie asked.

I shook my head. "I'm not lying, but I'm not sure I have a way to prove that to you."

She studied me before speaking again. "We're going to

take a recess to discuss all you've said. You seem sincere, but your story isn't all that believable." Her attention turned to the warlocks who'd escorted me into the room. "Take him back to his cell, and we'll call for him when we're ready."

Since I was heading back to the cell, I didn't think I'd hear from them any time soon. There would likely be an argument about whether they should trust a word I'd said and more arguments on whether it mattered if any of what I'd said was true. I'd broken a lot of laws, even if I wasn't actively working with rebels.

As I walked by, I caught Nicolas's smirk. I expected to see him shortly after I got back to my cell. He hadn't liked being chastised during the hearing, and since he couldn't take his anger out on anyone on the justice panel, I'd pay the price.

Chapter Three

I didn't look up right away when I heard the door to the detention area open since I expected it to be Nicolas. When no one taunted me or started making threats, I looked up to find Ambrose watching me.

I stood and met his gaze as several beats of silence passed.

"Sorry I didn't come to see you earlier," he finally said. "I tried, but they wouldn't let me in, and then Father sent me away."

"I understand," I assured him.

"Why did you lie to me about Juliet?"

"We're hunters," I replied with a shrug. "Under normal circumstances, I wouldn't have offered to help Juliet. I *shouldn't* have offered to help her, and I knew everyone would tell me I was wrong for doing it. There's just something about her. She makes me see the world in a whole new way. She makes me see how wrong I was about her kind."

"I was shocked to learn the truth," he admitted. "She doesn't seem like an animal. It was easy believing she's a witch."

"Do spellcasters ever give any shapeshifters a chance to prove they're more than animals?" I asked. "Those who work at the trading posts probably have a slightly different view since they interact with shapeshifters in human form. We hunt them and force them to stay in their animal form so other spellcasters can use them. They're drained until there's nothing left."

Ambrose cringed. "What we do isn't that bad. You make it sound like we're enslaving familiars."

I'd been on the other side of this conversation when I'd first met Juliet, and now I felt foolish for my earlier beliefs.

"This is crazy," I muttered.

"Which part?" Ambrose asked. "Or have you realized the whole thing is crazy?"

"It's all crazy," I admitted. "I haven't known Juliet long, and she changed views I've held my entire life. Of course, I'd never spent any real time around shapeshifters before meeting her."

"We spend a big part of our lives around familiars," Ambrose argued.

"We capture them and bring them back here in animal form," I pointed out. "All our experiences are with them in the worst possible situations, and I'd never spoken to one before Juliet. She was the first one I'd ever seen in human form. How is that possible? They have two sides, yet we only see one."

"With good reason," Ambrose stated. "Look what happened the first time you spoke to one. We can't do our job if we start worrying about how it affects them."

"It's not right," I stated.

"Keeping our distance from those we might need to kill?" he asked.

I nodded. "Yes, it makes it easier to kill them if we only look at the differences between shapeshifters and spellcasters, never the similarities."

"Life is simpler that way," he argued.

"That doesn't make it right, Ambrose."

He let out a frustrated breath. "This is worse than just not being able to do your job. You threw away your life and lied to your family for a familiar."

"Do you think of Juliet as nothing more than an animal?" I asked.

He shook his head. "I wish I did. When I heard about what she really is, I thought Nicolas was lying. Juliet seemed so much like us."

"She is like us," I told him. "Sure, there are differences, but there are differences between each family. We all have our unique gifts."

"We don't turn into animals," he pointed out.

"I know Juliet isn't *what* you believed she was, but she's still *who* you thought she was. She saved my life at significant risk to herself. Juliet could have left me to die and found her way to the rebels. That would have been safer for her than returning to Azuredale. Bringing her here put her in so much danger."

"But you didn't see any way around it," he added quietly. "You wouldn't have brought her here had you not believed it was the only way to keep her safe. You're a planner."

"I didn't have time to plan this situation with Juliet," I said with a bark of laughter. "I have this strong connection to her. We belong together."

"And you were willing to risk everything because of that connection," he grumbled. "You threw it all away."

"She's worth it. I'm sorry I had to lie to you, Ambrose. You're my brother, and I love you."

"But you also love her," he added with a sad smile.

"I do."

He nodded. "I'm not angry with you, Dante. At first, I was a little angry, but mostly I was hurt that you didn't come to me. Now, I see why you didn't. Do you think Serena will be okay? She's so fragile and terrified of shapeshifters. Will Juliet be able to protect her?"

"Serena isn't exactly defenseless," I reminded him. "I should have done something to stop Nicolas from tormenting her."

"We all should have," Ambrose agreed. "I tried pretending nothing was happening because I didn't want

Nicolas's attention focused on me, but that was selfish."

"We both screwed up," I stated. "Serena will be fine. The shapeshifter with her and Juliet owes me his life."

"I hope your trust in the rebel isn't misplaced, though I suppose you didn't think you had any other choice in that situation either."

"I didn't," I replied. "Of course, I didn't anticipate coming back here and being accused of plotting with the rebels. I thought I'd just be facing charges for helping Juliet and freeing Serena."

"Something tells me you still would have sacrificed yourself for Juliet," he remarked. "I suppose at least if you die, you'll do it with no regrets."

"I wouldn't go that far," I said with a bark of laughter. "There are a lot of things I wish I'd done differently, but I don't regret helping Juliet and Serena escape."

"You will," Nicolas said with a cheerful smile as he made his way into the room.

"Don't even think about touching my brother," Ambrose snarled.

Nicolas quirked an eyebrow, looking thoroughly amused. "What? No love for me? No love for your big brother?"

"Not when you've come in here to torture Dante," Ambrose told him. "I know you're responsible for his injuries."

"Dante was injured trying to escape." Nicolas was starting to look angry. "Are you taking the side of this traitor? Maybe someone should look into your loyalties as well."

"You know Ambrose isn't part of this," I told Nicolas. "He came to get answers from me."

"And did you get them?" Nicolas asked Ambrose. "Did our baby brother confess all his sins?"

"I'm not playing games with you," Ambrose snapped. "You got what you wanted. Dante will no longer be a threat to you, so let's go."

Nicolas didn't look like he intended to leave, and I was

starting to worry about Ambrose getting in trouble.

"You should go," I told Ambrose.

"I'll leave with Nicolas," Ambrose replied.

Nicolas's eyes narrowed. "I would hate to have to break Laranissa's heart by having another of her sons arrested, but your behavior is very suspicious."

"Imagine how suspicious it would look if a third member of our family was implicated," I mused. "The entire Verdugo family could end up under investigation, including you."

Nicolas glared at me as his jaw clenched so tightly that I saw the muscle tick on one side. "Fine," he bit out. "We're leaving. You'll be dead soon anyway."

Ambrose cast me a sad smile before leaving me alone.

Much as I appreciated the reprieve, something told me Nicolas was right; I didn't have much longer to live.

Chapter Four

It had been several hours since I'd been sent back to my cell, and I'd started to suspect my sentence wouldn't be announced until the next day.

I wasn't sure if I should consider it a good or bad sign that it was taking them so long to decide. It could mean that not all of the panel members were convinced I should die, or it could mean they hadn't agreed on a method of execution.

A guard brought me a small meal after Ambrose convinced Nicolas to leave, but I barely touched it. Instead, I laid on my cot and stared at the door.

As the hours ticked by, I realized Ambrose must have found a way to keep Nicolas from returning. I was grateful for the reprieve since I needed time to recover.

I let out a humorless laugh at my ridiculous thoughts.

Time to recover before I died?

I still appreciated the break from Nicolas's torture, though it gave me too much time alone with my thoughts.

My separation from Juliet felt more unnerving the longer I was away from her. It was as if a piece of me was missing.

No one had ever mentioned a familiar bond resulting in any kind of separation anxiety. Had that been the case, spellcasters would do more to keep their familiars alive.

The bond between two spellcasters was somewhat more complex, and I'd heard of them having separation issues. Few spellcasters entered into one of those bonds, most choosing a commitment ceremony instead. That's what my father had done with Laranissa.

As part of the bonding ceremony, each spellcaster had to give up a small piece of their magic to the other. The bound couple could sense each other even when they were apart. That had always sounded intrusive, but now I found myself wishing I could feel Juliet's presence in my mind.

Closing my eyes, I focused on her. While I could still sense the weak tendrils of our connection, I couldn't follow that connection to its source.

I longed to touch her magic, to feel her close to me even at a distance. Reaching out, I tried again to follow the link, but I hit a wall.

I let out a frustrated sigh. With the cuff suppressing my magic, I'd never be able to trace the link no matter how hard I tried. It said a lot about how strong our bond must be that I could sense it with the cuff on.

I stood and paced the cell, unable to handle the wait. Taking several deep breaths, I tried to think clearly.

Juliet had to be safe. If not, I wouldn't still sense our bond, or would I? If Juliet died, would I still feel that small bit of magic she'd shared with me?

No!

She had to be okay.

When the door opened, I froze, wondering if Nicolas had returned.

"Dinner time!" a warlock I'd never met announced as he entered the room with a tray.

He was much older than the others working in the detention areas, already having gray hair and lines on his face. It took at least two-hundred years for spellcasters to age that much.

"It hasn't been that long since I ate," I remarked suspiciously as he slid the tray through the slot in the bars.

"This is better than what you had earlier," he told me.

It certainly smelled better than the lukewarm soup I'd had earlier. I was also hungry, having barely touched that soup.

"I'm surprised you ended up in a mess like this, Dante."

"Have we met before?" I asked, making no move to grab the tray.

"No, but I've heard enough about you," he replied. "Eat your dinner. You'll need your strength for what's to come."

"My execution?" I asked with a wry smile as I finally grabbed the tray and set it on the small table.

He quirked an eyebrow. "You're sure you'll be executed?"

"Considering the charges against me, that's what I expect. I suppose they might consider my reasons and give me a lighter sentence."

"I wouldn't hold my breath on that," he said with a bark of laughter. "You're guilty of enough crimes that no one cares much about your motives. They want to make an example of you. Besides, no one wants you to share your new thoughts on how spellcasters have wronged shapeshifters."

"Azureans don't use the term *shapeshifter*," I said with narrowed eyes.

He smiled and nodded. "No, they don't. Now, eat. As I said before, you'll need your strength."

He left without giving me a chance to respond.

I stared at the tray.

I didn't know if I should trust the warlock. Something about him seemed off. He hadn't acted like the other guards.

I let out a bark of laughter and shook my head.

It was crazy to be paranoid about the guard's motives.

What was the worst he could do to me?

Poison me?

I was going to die anyway, so I decided I might as well enjoy a nice meal.

Chapter Five

Even before I opened my eyes, I knew I was no longer in my cell.

No dampening spell restrained my magic, and the mattress beneath me was much too comfortable. I also felt warm as if sunlight was coming in through the window.

This had to be a dream.

That was my first thought. Either that or the food really had been poisoned, and I'd passed on to the next realm. The lingering pain in my shoulder and ribs made that last unlikely.

Opening my eyes, I looked around the room. Sunlight streamed through a crack in the cream-colored curtains. There was a small dresser across from the bed. Paintings of trees and flowers hung on the walls. I looked to my side and saw a glass of water on the bedside table.

I definitely wasn't in my cell, which made no sense.

How had I gotten here?

Where exactly was I?

The last thing I clearly remembered was eating. After that, things got fuzzy.

I'd felt so drowsy that I'd had to lie down just before everything went black. My last fleeting thought had been that they'd decided to execute me with poison without telling me.

I'd been drugged, though I had no clue why. No one would have needed to drug me to convince me to move to a nicer location.

I sat up slowly, expecting the pain from my injuries to be much greater. Either I'd been unconscious for several days, or a healer had worked on me while I slept. I rolled my injured shoulder, cringing slightly.

Walking to the window, I pulled the curtains to the side and looked out. Two young children were playing just outside. There were other homes nearby, all much smaller than the family estates in Azuredale.

The door opened, and I turned quickly to face the older warlock who'd brought me the drugged food.

"You're finally awake." He sounded irritated by how long I'd been unconscious.

"Yes," I replied. "Where am I? Obviously, I'm no longer in Azuredale."

"No, you'd probably already be dead had I left you there." He sat on the only chair in the room. "This has been one heck of a week! When my daughter got placed in Azuredale, I figured we'd get updates, none of them good. After my witch reported back on meeting Serena, I decided there was hope for one Verdugo, but not the rest of you. You've surprised me, Dante."

"And you've confused me," I admitted. "Do you have a spy in the Verdugo household?"

"You're lucky we do, or you might already be dead," he replied. "With no one defending you, the only question left in the minds of the justice panel was how to execute you."

"Yeah, I know. There are a couple of people in my family who believe in my innocence, but that wouldn't have helped me. All their defense would have done was land them in trouble as well."

"Laranissa already told Ambrose to keep any defense of you to himself," he told me. "My daughter couldn't stand losing both of you. She's always loved you and Ambrose. It made it much harder to do her job. She also loves Nicolas, though I don't understand why."

"Wait! Laranissa is your daughter? She's the spy in the Verdugo family?"

I had to have misunderstood him. Sure, my stepmother had never quite fit in with our family, and her relationship with my father had never made any sense. That didn't mean I'd have ever suspected her of spying on us.

"Yes, she's my only child. It was easy getting her in there," he stated. "Your father wanted a biddable witch to help raise his children, and Laranissa makes no demands of him. I wasn't happy about her being there, but she's always been stubborn, much like her mother."

"Why are you telling me this?" I asked. "Aren't you worried I'll blow Laranissa's cover? You don't know me."

"I know you can't go back to Azuredale without getting yourself killed. Now that you've disappeared, you look even more guilty."

"Good point," I agreed. "How did you get me out of there? I know you drugged my food, but I'm not sure how you got into the detention area."

"We have people all over Azuredale," he explained. "It wasn't all that hard getting you out of there. Had Serena been in any real danger, we would have removed her from Azuredale after her arrest."

I could argue that she had been in danger from Nicolas. Laranissa had to have told her family about how he tormented Serena, unless she hadn't realized the extent of Serena's abuse. Still, it was possible they only considered loss of life a threat great enough to risk taking someone from Azuredale.

He was watching me intently. "Why did you risk your life for the shapeshifter?"

"Which one?" I asked.

His eyebrows shot up. "There was more than one shapeshifter?

"How do you think we found a shapeshifter willing to help us when we ran?" I asked.

"I assumed the female you helped escape knew the local rebels. I figured she was one of theirs," he admitted. "I thought your change of heart happened after you met the female shapeshifter. When did you help the other shapeshifter escape? How many have you helped?"

"Just the two. My change of heart did happen after I met Juliet," I told him. "I was supposed to kill a shapeshifter named Alaric the day after I brought Juliet to Azuredale. I couldn't do it with her watching me, so I faked his death and let him go. Juliet told me he'd rather die than end up a slave. I never used to think of the familiar practice as slavery."

"Because you're an idiot," he snapped.

"Are you going to tell me your name?" I asked.

"Edmond," he replied. "Since I've told everyone you're my grandson, you can call me Pops."

I nodded. "Thank you for saving me."

"Laranissa would have been crushed if you'd been executed. Do you think Serena is safe? Laranissa told me the girl is terrified of shapeshifters. If she decides to leave them, it will probably cost Serena her life. We won't have time to rescue her if she's captured, and with her history, it won't take long to order her execution."

"I'm pretty sure she'll stay with Juliet. I trust Juliet to look after her. Not to mention, Alaric owes me, and he agreed to protect Serena. He seems honorable."

He nodded. "Let's hope you're right. Your kind never appreciated her."

"Why do you refer to them as *my kind* when we're both spellcasters?" I asked.

"Because you grew up with the idiots of the magical world," he snapped. "You've all been fed some ridiculous story about how the shapeshifters came into being. Laranissa was the only good influence in your life, and she could only correct the misinformation you'd been fed so much without giving away her secret. She couldn't tell you the truth about how shapeshifters came into being."

"Are you saying the story Juliet told me is true?" I

asked. "Did the spell take on a life of its own and result in the birth of the shapeshifters?"

He let out a bark of laughter. "Magic doesn't behave that way, boy. Those are just stories told to scare youngsters into being cautious with their spellcasting. The spell was intentionally altered by the first rebels—a group of spellcasters who realized what we were doing was wrong."

My mouth dropped open. Though that explanation made more sense than the spell taking on a life of its own or the familiars learning how to steal our magic to alter the spell, I still found it hard to believe.

"How did they alter the spell so dramatically without triggering any warnings?" I asked.

"Let's have that discussion during lunch," he suggested. "Our food is getting cold. This time, I promise I won't drug you."

He walked out, and after a brief pause, I followed him.

I was dying to hear the rest of his story.

Chapter Six

I didn't learn much more about how the original spell was altered during lunch. It's not that Pops refused to answer my questions. He tried, but the two young witches I'd seen outside my window had an endless string of questions for me.

I learned that Pops lived alone, but the children he taught in the afternoon joined him for lunch each day. These young witches, Tori and Loni, were at his house two days a week. A large gray and white dog sniffed around my legs during the meal.

Tori had bronzed skin, pale green eyes, and long silky brown hair. Loni was incredibly pale with freckles, brown eyes, and short red hair.

Every time I thought they'd run out of questions, a new round started.

"Were you scared when you thought you might die?" Tori asked with a mouth full of food.

"Yes," I admitted.

"Was it the part about dying or the pain?" Loni asked.

I thought for a moment before responding. "The pain scared me more, but I was also afraid of leaving behind people who still need me."

"Like the shapeshifter you helped?" Tori asked.

I nodded. "And my cousin. I'm still very worried about them."

"You were willing to die for them," Tori said with a sigh.

"Because you're a hero," Loni added.

"There are no heroes," Pops said as he waved a fork at her.

"That's not true," I argued. "My cousin, Serena, is a hero. She was terrified, and she knew she would get into a lot of trouble, but she still rescued Juliet."

"She must be very brave," Loni mused. "I get scared a lot."

"Me too," Tori added. "There's a lot to be afraid of. If anyone ever finds out we're here, they might kill us."

"You know that powerful spells woven into the Black Mist protect Reaper Ridge," Pops reminded them. "There's nothing to be afraid of. Only those we invite here can pass through the Black Mist. Even if that weren't the case, I think it's a stretch to believe we'd be killed for living away from the other spellcasters. We aren't the only remote settlement."

"But we have a lot of enemies who want us dead," Tori argued.

"Who told you that?" Pops asked with narrowed eyes.

"Ariana told us during our lesson yesterday," Loni explained. "She said if the other spellcasters found out we're here, there would be a war."

Pops snorted. "Ariana is only saying that so you'll work harder on your defensive spells. Only those who have to travel beyond the Black Mist are in danger."

"Like our spies?" Tori asked.

Pops nodded. "Exactly! If you decide to become spies or scouts, you'll be in danger."

I didn't agree that they had nothing to worry about. All it took was one traitor to bring the enemy to their door, but Pops probably realized that as well. He was likely telling the young witches what they needed to hear to feel safe.

"I didn't know anyone lived anywhere near Reaper

Ridge," I remarked. "When I was a child, I was told that demons guard the ridge, and I'd better stay away if I value my life."

It had been years since I'd believed in the existence of demons. While there were several creatures I'd never seen, I knew at least one spellcaster who could claim to have had some sort of encounter with them.

That wasn't the case with demons. No one I knew had ever seen one. As a child, I'd tried to imagine what they might look like, coming up with all sorts of nightmarish ideas. As I'd gotten older, I'd stopped believing in their existence.

"It's smart for the Azureans to stay away from demons," Pops stated. "We have a special arrangement so they won't hurt us. The ones around here won't bother you."

My mouth dropped open, and I just stared at him, figuring he'd tell me he was joking. When he simply continued eating, I asked, "Demons really exist?"

"Of course, silly," Loni replied with a giggle.

"And you've interacted with them?" I asked as I looked between the three.

"You have to if you live here," Pops replied.

"They like it when you rub their bellies," Tori added.

"Rub their bellies?" I asked slowly.

"Don't worry too much about demons," Pops told me. "They mostly keep to themselves, especially with newcomers. I've found that they're more dangerous around those they don't trust, so you should just avoid them."

"What do they look like?" I asked. "I can't avoid them if I don't know what I'm looking for."

"They can take on any shape," Loni replied with a giggle as she looked over at the dog who'd been watching me throughout the meal.

"That's a demon?" I gestured to the dog.

Pops shook his head. "No, but a lot of demons take on the form of a dog. This dog hates all other dogs, so if you see her around one, it's a demon. Be careful what you say around her since this old girl's a gossip. I found that out the hard way. Anything I say about demons, she passes on to them."

"They speak dog?" I asked.

"They can communicate with just about any living creature, from what I can tell," Pops explained.

"I'll just avoid dogs to be on the safe side," I replied.

"Good plan," Pops agreed.

"What exactly do you do out here, other than send spies to different areas?" I asked.

"Much like in Azuredale, we all have our roles to play in making sure things run smoothly. A lot of us go out and try to release shapeshifters from traps before hunters find them."

"I always thought that was other shapeshifters," I mused. "It made me wonder how some of the rebels had learned to disrupt our spells."

"I don't think they can do anything like that," he replied. "We don't exactly talk to them when we release them since they're in animal form and more concerned with getting out of the area than figuring out why we let them go. That's our biggest concern as well. When we go out, we don't want any hunters finding us releasing their prey."

"I can help with that," I told him. "I know where all the traps are, and I know the hunting schedule."

"We already know the schedule," Pops replied. "How do you think we're able to release so many shapeshifters? We have to avoid the hunters when we need to pass through an area on that day's rotation. They don't always follow the same route when checking traps."

"I know how every last one of the Azurean hunters acts when they're out. New hunters are the only wildcards. The seasoned hunters follow a specific route every time they hunt. You saved my life, and I want to do something to pay you back."

Pops shook his head. "I'm not putting you out there when you're considered an even bigger prize for the hunters. We stuck our necks out to rescue you, so you stay here."

"I can't stay here forever," I insisted.

"Why not?" Tori asked. "It's nice here, and you'll be safe."

"The demons will get used to you," Loni added.

"I have to get to Juliet and Serena," I explained.

"They're both safe enough where they are," Pops told me.

"Juliet won't stay with the rebels long," I stated. "It's only a matter of time before she tries to find a way to get back to her home in the Heathergate Refuge. I can't let her face that danger alone."

"Pain in the neck warlock," Pops muttered.

"But you see why I can't stay here," I pushed.

"Because you're a hero," Tori said with a smile.

"Because he's a fool," Pops replied. "We'll talk about your plans later. For now, everyone needs to finish eating so I can get started on Tori and Loni's lessons."

"Can you tell me how the spell on the familiars was altered first?"

He gave me a one-word reply. "Demons."

Chapter Seven

By the end of my second week with Pops, I was going stir-crazy.

Don't get me wrong; I was grateful to still be alive and appreciated Pops for not only saving me but giving me a safe place to stay while I came up with a plan.

It's not as if I could just race off to find Juliet, especially while I was still recovering from my injuries. No matter how much my magic sped up the healing process, it still took time to mend broken bones and damaged tissue.

Planning during my recovery wasn't as easy as I'd have liked. Technology wasn't readily available to everyone. There were some computers and phones, but they were all in use most of the time. Those assigned as watchers used them to keep in contact with spies placed in other spellcaster communities. Others took them when they went out to release shapeshifters from traps.

The everyday life of the spellcasters living beyond the Black Mist didn't rely as much on technology. They had basic appliances to make life easier, but their focus was more on magic and the power of nature.

Each day, groups of two to six young spellcasters came to the house around lunchtime for training.

Unlike in Azuredale, children went from house to

house to learn. They didn't focus on just their strengths; they were challenged in areas of weakness. Every community member was expected to have training in all areas of magic, and children were allowed to choose their path, within reason. They had to have some aptitude in the type of magic needed.

Since Pops had six young warlocks in his home that afternoon, I decided to explore on my own for the first time.

The homes and yards were small. Everyone went to the community areas to connect with nature if they wanted to stay close to home.

I was walking among the trees in a park at the center of the settlement when I noticed a large black dog following me. I'd seen her hanging around Pops's house, but she'd never come near me.

I decided to explore farther out and headed toward the edge of the community. No one stopped me, something I'd worried might happen, even after Pops said I wasn't a prisoner.

Away from the homes and other buildings, I walked across an open field and stopped to look out to where I could clearly see the protection spell. It was like nothing I'd ever seen before.

"Why are you following me?" I asked without turning to look at the dog.

There was no logical reason to assume she was anything other than an ordinary dog, yet something told me this was a demon. The children called her Sin, and I'd noticed her unnerving stare fixed on me several times.

She moved around in front of me and rolled onto her back, waiting for me to rub her belly. Crouching down, I stroked her soft fur, and magic vibrated up my arm. I continued to rub her belly as the energy became uncomfortable, moving along my skin like pins and needles.

When she changed to a beautiful woman with long blood-red hair, dressed in a white sundress, I tried jerking away. She caught my wrist in her surprisingly firm grip and held my hand over her belly as she arched up and let out a sound like a purr.

Tiny fangs hung over the top of her lower lip when she smiled, and her deep red eyes danced with amusement. Her skin was several shades lighter than mine and looked almost like porcelain.

"Why did you stop rubbing, warlock?" Her voice was soft and melodic, filled with power that sent tingles up my spine.

"I'm not comfortable rubbing your belly under these circumstances," I explained as I tried pulling my hand away again.

Her laughter washed over my skin, raising goosebumps in its wake. I knew it wasn't so much the sound as it was the magic in her voice. I'd never been around a more powerful creature. Her presence was both unnerving and fascinating.

"Don't you like me, warlock?" she asked with an impish smile. "Am I not as pretty as the witches you know?"

"I don't know you well enough to like you," I replied. "I also don't believe you doubt your beauty."

"But do *you* think I'm beautiful?"

"Yes." I looked at her delicate hand that had a vice grip around my wrist. "Can I have my hand back, Sin?"

She released my hand and smiled. "You know my name!"

I nodded as I rubbed my hand, still feeling the pins and needles sensation from her magic. "Yes, I've heard your name and seen you around the house. I'm Dante."

"I know who you are," she replied with another laugh. "Why else would I follow you?"

I shrugged, still crouching close to her. "For all I know, you could be bored or curious."

"I *am* curious, warlock. You're a hunter, a killer. I've heard about what you did, and I wanted to see for myself if you're an honorable warlock or if you're going to betray us.

We don't bring in many outsiders."

"That's smart," I agreed.

"You're a very interesting warlock, and I think we can trust you," she said with a wave of her hand as she sat up and scooted closer.

"And how do you know that?"

"When you touched me, I probed a little. You're not plotting against us."

"You read my mind? Can all demons do that when they touch someone else?"

"Read your mind?" she asked with a laugh. "I can't enter your mind without your permission. What I can read is your intent, for lack of a better word. You're angry and want revenge, but that anger is directed far from here."

Some spellcasters were powerful empaths, so her explanation made sense.

She studied me as if I were some exotic creature she'd never seen before. "After I heard your story, I was mildly curious. It's why I started following you. You're more interesting than I first thought."

"Why is that? I haven't done much since I got here."

"When I touched your magic, I felt both spellcaster and shapeshifter," she replied as she regarded me with a more serious expression. "Are you part shapeshifter, warlock?"

"You can call me by my name," I said rather than answering her question.

"You should hope I forget your name. Telling someone your name gives them a certain amount of power over you. It's why we demons never share our names."

"But I already know your name."

She quirked a thin red eyebrow. "You think Sin is my real name? It's just what the children call me. Some of the other demons know my real name, but only the ones I trust with my very existence. Spellcasters are careless and share their real names with every creature they meet."

"Are you planning to use my name to harm me?"

"You can trust me," she assured me with a sweet smile.

"Unless I'm lying about you being able to trust me. You never can tell with a demon. Do I frighten you?"

I shrugged as I stood. "You make me a little uneasy, but I wouldn't say you scare me."

"You're ruining my fun," she accused with a frown. "Why do you have to be so difficult?"

"How am I ruining your fun?"

"I only made you jump once," she complained as she stood and moved closer again.

"I didn't expect you to change forms," I admitted.

"Did you know what I am?"

I nodded. "I suspected you were a demon before I touched you. The way your magic behaved made me more certain. I've never felt anything like it. How is it that you're fully clothed? Shapeshifters are naked when they go from animal to human form."

"It's an illusion, like the dog form." When she waved a hand in front of herself, the dress's color changed from white to pale blue.

"So, you don't actually look like this?" I asked. "This is all an illusion?"

"Some of it," she replied. "Parts of this form are real. The clothing is all illusion. I normally remain in dog form around spellcasters. It's easier that way."

"Because you don't have to wear clothes?" I asked.

"I don't mind that part," she insisted. "It's talking to spellcasters that I prefer to avoid. The conversations can become tedious, especially with the young ones who are full of questions."

I also had quite a few questions.

"Are you part shapeshifter?" she asked.

I shook my head. "No. Didn't you say you'd already heard my story?"

"Bits and pieces," she replied. "I get bored easily, so I didn't stick around for the entire story."

"Then I suppose I should skip telling you everything."

"Give me the highlights," she prompted.

"My magic is somehow joined with the shapeshifter I

rescued," I explained.

"The Azurean spellcasters must have been furious." She sounded excited by the prospect.

"They were going to execute me."

"That seems a bit harsh just for binding your magic to a shapeshifter," she remarked.

"I think they were more upset about me lying and helping her escape," I explained. "My brother convinced them I'd been plotting with rebel shapeshifters."

Her expression turned sympathetic as she regarded me. "I have a brother like that. He's always stirring up trouble."

"Does he live here?"

She shook her head. "No, he's not allowed in this area. It's one of the reasons I like it so much here. It's strange that you were able to bind your magic to a shapeshifter's. That shouldn't be possible."

"That's what I thought," I agreed. "It turns out we were both mistaken."

"Unless one of you is not what you seem." She studied me before continuing. "Now that I know what I'm sensing, it's obvious the shapeshifter magic isn't yours. Your shapeshifter may have some spellcaster blood."

"No, she doesn't," I insisted.

"And you know this how?" she asked.

"I didn't sense spellcaster magic," I explained.

"You could have missed it if her shapeshifter side is more dominant," she argued. "There's likely been more intermingling between spellcasters and shapeshifters than anyone knows."

"What makes you sure my power couldn't have bound itself to hers some other way? Shapeshifters bond with spellcasters as part of the familiar process."

"Yes, but that's a forced bonding," she insisted. "Did you force her to give you part of her magic while she was in animal form?"

"Of course not. I'm not sure how it happened," I admitted. "I am certain I didn't simply take part of her magic. It felt as if I gave her power as well. I've never experienced anything like it, but I've also never had a familiar."

"This doesn't sound anything like how I've heard the familiar bond described," she insisted. "What you're saying isn't possible unless a demon has somehow altered the spell used to create shapeshifters."

"Why would a demon have needed to alter it?" I asked.

"Shapeshifters are the result of demon magic. Some spellcasters were also involved, but it was mostly demons. We're much more powerful."

"Of course," I agreed. "Pops told me demons were involved with the creation of shapeshifters. I would have laughed if someone told me this a week ago."

"Because you didn't believe in demons?" she asked.

I nodded. "Exactly. Why did demons get involved?"

"Since we often stay in animal form, we felt more empathy for familiars. Demons also don't like most spellcasters. You are an arrogant species. A group of less arrogant spellcasters approached us with the idea of altering the familiar spell. We originally hoped that if spellcasters saw the shapeshifters in human form, they'd see that keeping a familiar was wrong."

"That's an interesting story," I mused.

"You don't believe me?" she demanded. "Didn't I tell you that you can trust me?"

"You also made it sound like I may not be able to trust you," I pointed out. "I think I'll reserve judgment until I've known you a bit longer, but I believe your story about demons helping modify the spell. It makes more sense than any other explanation I've heard."

Her smile turned wistful as her eyes closed. "You're quite smitten with the shapeshifter, aren't you? It's why you sacrificed everything for her."

I quirked an eyebrow. "Smitten? That's a very romantic way to describe my feelings for Juliet."

She frowned as she studied me. "Such a disappointing response. I'd hoped to hear about your grand romance with the shapeshifter you would die for. It would be proof that we can bridge the gap between your two species. I'm growing impatient with both species. Your stupid fighting is a complete waste of time after we put so much effort into making things perfect for you."

"Perfect?" I asked. "I would hardly describe our situation as perfect. If our situation were perfect, we wouldn't have rebel communities, and I wouldn't have grown up learning to kill Juliet's kind. There's nothing perfect about any of this."

Sin's face flushed with anger. "You are stupid, warlock!" she shouted. "That is the biggest problem with your kind. We gave you the tools to make a better world, but you never do anything with them. You have an entire continent free of non-magical humans. Do you ever thank us? No. Instead, you tell stories about the mighty wars your kind fought." She snorted before continuing. "I like the spellcasters that live here, but the rest of you make me regret giving you this land."

Wow!

She'd revealed a lot of information.

Sin shifted to dog form and took off running, leaving me wondering if she'd seek me out again.

Chapter Eight

After Sin stormed off, I expected her to avoid me, at least for a short time.

I had to wait for Pops to finish his lessons that day before I could talk to him about my conversation with her.

He looked thoughtful as he pondered what I'd told him. "That's strange. I wouldn't have expected her to let you see her in human form, but I suppose it's the only way she could communicate with you."

"Do you think she'll avoid me now?" I asked. "She didn't seem happy with my response."

He shrugged. "You'll know soon enough. One thing I've noticed about demons is they either hold a grudge for the rest of your days, or they forget they're mad at you almost instantly."

Sin showed up at Pops's place in dog form a short time later and started following me around again. I got very little time to myself over the next two days.

The demon loved having her belly rubbed, and she often blocked my path until I gave in. Touching her was still unnerving, but not so much as the first time.

"Does the demon magic bother you?" I asked Pops as I pushed my food around on my plate. My gaze was locked with Sin's as she sat on the floor, watching me.

"Bother me how?" he asked.

"Does it feel weird?"

He looked at Sin and then at me. "I've never felt demon magic that I'm aware of. That's not true. There is a slight buzzing in the air when they change forms, but I've only been around a few for that. Is that what you're talking about?"

I shook my head. "When I rub Sin's belly, I feel her power moving along my skin."

"Huh. That's strange. I've only heard of that happening when a demon takes a spellcaster as a mate."

"Mate? No, that can't be it. We only talked for a few minutes, and I didn't get that vibe from her."

Sin cocked her head to the side. It would be nice to know what she was thinking, but she didn't seem interested in changing forms.

"I'm not looking for a mate," I stated. "Juliet is the only one for me."

Pops shrugged. "If Sin thought you were her mate, she'd have changed forms to tell you so, unless she's angry and planning to get her revenge later. That's always possible."

"I suppose I'll find out soon enough," I replied.

Sin yawned and rested her chin on her front paws as if bored with our conversation already.

"What are your plans for today?" Pops asked. "It seems you're feeling up to helping out more around here."

"I'm almost fully recovered from my injuries, so it's time to start making plans for me to leave," I replied. "Of course, I'm also glad to take on some work. I owe you all a great debt."

"Leave? And do what?" Pops asked. "Do you want to get yourself killed after I went to such great lengths to save you? Is that what you're hoping to do?"

"I can't stay here forever," I told him.

"Why not?" he asked. "If living with me is a problem, we can find you a place. I promised my daughter I'd keep you safe."

"I appreciate all you've done for me, but I have to get to Juliet. It feels like I'm being torn in two." I took a deep breath and released it as I tried to find a way to explain how I felt. "Juliet is a part of me. I constantly feel the draw of her magic. It's torture not being able to reach out and touch her mind. I wake up in a cold sweat, having dreamt of her death. Even if it weren't for the magical bond between us, I need to get to her because I love her. I can't let anything happen to her."

Pops looked irritated. "You think I don't know how hard it is to be separated from someone you love? Not a day goes by that I don't miss my witch and daughter, but there's nothing I can do for them."

"Our situations are totally different," I argued. "You have responsibilities here. Yes, you can assign me some jobs to help out, but you don't need me here."

"Laranissa will be heartbroken if anything happens to you," he said with a sigh. "My daughter has given up so much for the cause."

"I love Laranissa, and I don't want to hurt her, but she's not the only one I need to worry about. I can't stay here."

Pops fell silent. He'd been good to me, but I wasn't certain if he liked me or merely wanted to make his daughter happy. That is until I saw the genuine emotion in his eyes.

"You know, Dante, I didn't expect to like you. My daughter even tries to find nice things to say about Nicolas, and he's a lost cause. Her love for you clouds her judgment, but she was right. You're a good warlock, and I can see why she defends you. It's one of the reasons I'd like you to stay. It would be safer if you built a new life for yourself here, but I understand why you can't. I'm not sure I'd respect you as much if you could abandon Juliet and Serena."

"I wouldn't respect myself," I told him.

"I'd rather respect you less and have you stay. You'll probably get yourself killed."

Sin's growl drew both our attention.

"We'd better save this talk for later," Pops suggested. "It's upsetting the demon, and they can be vicious when riled. It's important to keep them calm."

"Did the demons help with the protection spells here?"

"Yes, demon and spellcaster magic was involved. They've lived among us for centuries, and we've developed a rapport with them. I think it's similar to the relationship we were meant to have with shapeshifters. Neither is master over the other. We both need each other for survival."

"What do the demons need from spellcasters?" I asked. "It seems they're the more powerful species."

"Nothing is ever as simple as it appears," Pops replied. "Since this isn't my explanation to give, I'll let you try to get it out of your demon friend."

"So, you think she's my friend?" I asked.

"I don't know what to think," he admitted. "She's been here since before I was born, and she usually keeps to herself. This is the most I've ever seen of her, so I have to assume she likes being around you."

"Except when I make her angry enough to yell at me and storm off," I replied with a laugh.

"Demons are impulsive and hot-tempered," he began. "Since she returned, it's proof she wasn't really angry with you. I still think she might consider you her mate."

"I don't see it."

He shrugged before looking down at Sin who was still watching us. "I'm not going to rule out the possibility. If you're lucky, she's following you because she likes you. If not, you might want to start sucking up to her before she kills you in your sleep."

Pops grabbed his empty dish and headed toward the sink.

I looked down at Sin. "Are you going to tell me why you follow me everywhere?"

Her only response was to roll onto her back and wait for me to rub her belly.

Chapter Nine

It was the middle of the night when I heard my bedroom door open just before a shadowy figure slipped into my room. The moment I saw her face, I knew I was dreaming.

Juliet couldn't possibly be there, yet I still felt relief when I saw her approaching the bed.

She looked so beautiful as the flecks of gold in her green eyes seemed to sparkle. Her long black hair was tied back from her face, and I could swear I even caught her scent in the air.

I dreamt of her nightly, but this was the first time she'd come so close to me. It felt much more real than the other dreams and disjointed nightmares I'd had about her death.

I sat up and reached out a hand to her. "I've missed you, Juliet," I whispered.

She smiled, and her hand went straight through mine. Looking down at her hand, which appeared solid, she frowned. "Why can't I touch you?"

"Because you're a dream," I told her with a sad sigh. "I don't know how to get to you, but I'm coming as soon as I have a plan. I have to find a way to avoid being recaptured by the Azureans."

"You should probably stay here," she stated as she looked around the room. "It's not safe for you to travel when they're looking for you."

"If you were truly my Juliet, you'd know I can't do that. I can't stay away from you."

"That was mean."

"Saying I can't stay away from you?"

She shook her head and sat on the edge of the bed. "Saying I'm not your Juliet."

"I'm arguing with my dream," I said with a soft chuckle.

She looked over to where Sin lay asleep on the floor. "You have a dog. Do they keep them as pets where you're at?"

"They do, but that's a demon, not a dog."

She started to laugh, but her expressions sobered when she realized I wasn't joking. "This is my strangest dream about you so far."

"I'm the one dreaming about you," I reminded her.

"You sound so much like my Dante. Is the demon your friend?"

"I don't know," I admitted. "She's not speaking to me, or I'd ask her. She follows me everywhere, but she won't answer any of my questions."

"Maybe she's mad that you want to leave her to try finding me," she suggested.

"Why would she be mad about that?"

"If she likes you, then she may not want you to leave," Juliet replied. "You need to consider the feelings of those you leave behind."

My mind immediately went to Ambrose and Laranissa. Laranissa knew I was safe, but I doubted she'd share that information with Ambrose for fear of blowing her cover. My brother would never know what had happened to me unless I got caught.

Next, my mind went to Juliet. It had been around a month since I'd last seen her, and though I knew she'd gotten away with Alaric and Serena, I still worried she'd be captured.

"I hope you're safe, Juliet."

"I'm fine," she insisted. "You can see me right here."

"But you're just a dream," I reminded her. "You're miles away from me."

"Not for long," she assured me. "We'll be together soon. Can't you feel the tug of my magic? It's calling to you just as yours calls to me."

"I feel it every waking second," I replied. "Sometimes, I feel like I could follow the threads of our joined power back to you."

"I feel the same, and I've tried following the threads to you in my mind, but I always hit a wall, like you're hidden from me."

"The magic around Reaper Ridge probably interferes," I mused. "I wish you weren't just a dream."

"That's supposed to be my line," she argued. "I don't want to wake up, Dante. It's almost as if I have you back."

"I'm going to find you."

"We both know we may never see each other again," she said with a sad smile. Her eyes narrowed with annoyance as she looked around.

"What's wrong?" I asked.

"Someone is pounding on my door," she explained. "I'm not ready to wake up, not ready to leave you."

"Then don't," I coaxed as I reached out to brush her cheek only to meet with the sad reminder that I couldn't touch her. She wasn't there. "Stay a little longer. I'm not ready for this dream to end."

She was already fading. "I'm waking up, Dante. I miss you."

And then she was gone. I sat in the empty room and looked around. I could swear I caught a hint of her scent before a tongue on my cheek woke me.

I opened my eyes and glared at Sin, who was no longer in dog form as she licked my cheek.

"Why are you licking me?" I demanded.

"To wake you up," she replied with a grin before

licking me again.

"This got decidedly weirder," I muttered as I climbed out of bed and headed to the bathroom.

Chapter Ten

I washed my face before returning to have a talk with Sin about boundaries and personal space.

This wasn't the first time I'd had to talk to her about licking my face, but this was the first time she hadn't been in dog form. This was worse.

Though all the demons living among the spellcasters were very old, they were often childish and impulsive. They enjoyed playing with the children but rarely interacted with adults. I'd had several pointed out to me, and they behaved like beloved pets around the children.

Sin might not have realized it was even worse to lick my face in this form, but I wouldn't guarantee that was the case. She liked finding ways around any rules I set.

It was a game to her.

I said she couldn't climb into my bed *with* me, so she jumped onto my bed *before* me.

I told her to stay off my bed, so she tried jumping on top of me without touching the bed.

Pops had gotten a mattress to put on my bedroom floor since Sin seemed determined to sleep in my room, but she preferred my bed.

I'd dealt with everything from her getting into the shower with me to her eating my toothpaste.

When I returned to my bedroom, I found Sin sprawled out on my bed, dressed in one of my shirts. "Your clothes smell nice, but they're scratchy. I'm not used to wearing real clothes. Do you mind if I take your shirt off and hold it by my nose?"

"Keep the shirt on," I told her.

"You're such a prudish warlock," she said with a pout. "If you're bound to a shapeshifter, you should be used to nudity. She has to undress to change forms."

"That's different from you hanging out in my room naked," I argued.

"I'm always naked around you," she reminded me before looking at my shirt. "Except for now."

"Well, I don't always see you naked, and it doesn't count when you're in dog form. I'd really appreciate it if you kept the shirt on."

She let out an exasperated sigh and propped herself up on one elbow. "Fine, I'll keep the shirt on."

"Thank you," I replied. "Don't lick me in any form."

"Why not? I thought you didn't want my dog tongue on you."

"No tongue of any kind," I clarified.

She pouted. "Fine, then can I kiss you to wake you up next time?"

"No!"

"There's no reason to sound so horrified," she complained. "You like the way I look, and I'm sure you'd like kissing me. I'm very good at it. Well, I was the last time I tried. It's been a few years, maybe fifty or so."

"You're beautiful, but I love Juliet," I reminded her.

She looked perplexed by my answer. "What does that have to do with me kissing you? I'm not asking you to be my mate."

"It would be wrong," I told her.

"Spellcasters are so strange," she mused. "No matter how many decades I live among your kind, I don't understand your motivations. Kissing is fun. It's got nothing to do with love."

"It does for me. Juliet would not appreciate me kissing you or anyone else."

She huffed and sat up before swinging her legs over the side of the bed. "You're ruining my fun again, warlock! That's all you ever do! I start to have fun, and you ruin it for me!"

"Then why do you keep following me everywhere?" I asked.

She looked stricken.

"You want me to leave you alone?"

I shook my head. "I never said that. Just because I don't want to be licked or kissed by you doesn't mean I don't want you around. I don't want to be kissed or licked by Pops, but I like his company."

"Fine," she relented. "No kissing or licking."

"Are you going to tell me why you follow me around?"

She shrugged. "I like you."

"Even though I ruin your fun?" I asked.

"Who doesn't ruin my fun?" she shot back. "I'm so bored with my life here. How was your shapeshifter? You seemed agitated after your visit, and I think it was about more than me licking you."

"Visit?" I asked. "Juliet is far from here, so there was no visit, just another dream. This one was much more vivid."

Sin rolled her eyes. "You're so clueless."

"Are you saying that wasn't a dream?"

"It was," she replied before adding, "but it wasn't."

"That answer was needlessly confusing," I muttered. "Are you doing this on purpose?"

"Doing what?" she asked with wide, innocent eyes.

"Giving me little bits of information to confuse and frustrate me," I replied.

"I didn't realize that's what I was doing," she admitted. "Would you believe me if I told you it's because I haven't talked to anyone else in a very long time?"

"I might if you didn't sound like you're looking for an excuse that I'll believe," I said with a laugh. "Did you have something to do with my dream? All I want is a yes or no answer. You either had something to do with it or you didn't."

"Why do you always think things are black and white?" she asked. "The world is full of grays, and the failure of spellcasters to see that has caused the deaths of many shapeshifters."

"You're probably right, but don't change the subject. Was that a dream?"

"Yes, but you shared it with Juliet," she explained.

"How is that possible?"

"Since your magic is linked, I was able to pull your subconscious minds into the same plane."

"I've never heard of any spell that can control someone's dreams, and it seems impossible to share a dream."

"I don't use spells," she said around a yawn. "It's my magic. Of course, you've never heard of it. You didn't even believe in demons until recently."

"Why did you do this?" I asked.

She shrugged before lying down and curling up on her side. "You seemed upset. You call out her name in your sleep, and you always sound like your heart is breaking. I hate seeing you that way, so I decided it might make you feel better to see her tonight."

Her response to my pain genuinely surprised me. "Thank you, Sin, and I'm sorry for being so rude to you when you woke me up. I like you, too."

"Does this mean I can lick you again?" she asked. "You taste delicious."

I really hoped she didn't mean she wanted to eat me, but I decided against asking. "I still don't want you licking me."

"Fine," she agreed with a huff. "You can lick me if you want."

"Uh, thanks. Are you planning to sleep in my bed?"

Her eyes were already drifting shut. "Yes, I'm tired. Don't worry. I won't lick you."

I smiled as I watched the demon grab my pillow and hug it. "Now that I'm up, I'm going to do some planning while you sleep."

"What kind of planning?" she asked as she cracked an eye open to look at me.

"I'm going after Juliet soon."

"Good," she replied. "It's time for an adventure. We should leave soon."

"We?" I asked in surprise.

"You may ruin my fun most of the time, but you're still entertaining," she explained. "I'm going with you."

Chapter Eleven

My time for planning had been seriously limited in the last few days.

Pops had gotten me assigned to one of the teams patrolling the perimeter, so I was busy for several hours each day. I was happy to help more, but it made planning harder since I was exhausted most evenings. Patrolling involved even more walking than hunting.

This was the first day they'd let me go off on my own, and I suspected it was only because Sin kept growling at anyone who got close. She didn't seem to like any of the spellcasters they assigned to work with me.

I was walking along a narrow river with Sin by my side in dog form. Traveling this far out was against the rules, but I couldn't help myself.

Each day, the pull of Juliet's magic grew stronger. I hadn't quite passed through the magic in the Black Mist yet, but I was close enough that my connection to Juliet intensified with each step.

"You want to go after her now, don't you?" Sin asked, having changed forms while my back was to her.

I turned and nodded. "Yes. Do you think this is why they don't want me walking this far out? Is Pops afraid I'll take off without warning? Did he tell the others to keep me close?"

"He might be worried about that, but it's also more dangerous here because you can be seen from the other side of the Black Mist. The veil of magic is thinner. It's why you're drawn to this spot. Your link to the shapeshifter is stronger here."

"Why didn't anyone mention this to me before?" I asked. "This seems like the kind of thing they should have warned me about before letting me patrol alone."

I was more annoyed that no one had told me my link to Juliet would be stronger near the edge of the spell, even though I understood they'd likely kept that information from me to prevent me from traveling this far out.

She shrugged. "They probably thought that telling you it's dangerous was enough to keep you away from this area. You're not good at following orders."

"I used to be very good at following orders."

"That must have been boring," she mused. "I like you better this way. You think for yourself, but it might be smart to believe others when they tell you something is dangerous."

I nodded and looked around. "I should have asked for an explanation. All right, we'll head away from the edge of the spell."

I hesitated, not quite ready to move away from an area where my connection to Juliet felt stronger.

Just as I was about to start walking, I heard her voice.

"Dante? Is that you?"

"Juliet?" I asked.

"Have you lost your mind?" Sin asked as she looked around. "There's no one here but me."

"I heard her, but it must have been in my mind," I replied as I concentrated on the link between us.

"Juliet? Can you hear me?"

I was relieved when I heard her response in my mind.

"I hear you. Are you okay? I've been so afraid for you."

"I'm fine," I assured her. *"Are you okay?"*

"*Yes,*" she replied. *"I'm safe, but I miss you. I keep dreaming about you. Where are you?"*

As I was about to respond, I felt oily tendrils of energy slide along my bond with Juliet before it glided closer to me.

"I have to go," I told her urgently. *"I'll be coming for you soon."*

I turned, prepared to run, but it was too late.

Chapter Twelve

"Demon hunters!" Sin shouted before knocking me to the ground.

The air sizzled above my head as a wave of magic flowed past me. Burning pain spread throughout my entire body; I was nearly paralyzed by it and had to struggle to drag myself forward.

"We have to run!" She grabbed my arm and yanked me to my feet.

Run?

It was all I could do to stay on my feet under the weight of the heavy black magic pooling around us. I'd never experienced anything like this. I tried to speak, but my tongue felt like lead and wouldn't move. The magic was too much, and it was dragging me down.

Sin screamed as the shroud of dark magic grew thicker.

"Dante! Please!"

I still couldn't respond in words, but I focused on getting my feet to move as I dragged Sin along by my side since the magic seemed to hit her harder. I sensed the threat getting closer, even as my field of vision narrowed.

Focus or die!

Those were my only options, and I refused to go down

without a fight.

Dark, oily magic continued to flow around us, but this time, I focused on the power and its source as I tried to figure out a way to deal with it. When I pressed at the magic, it retreated slightly, easing the weight on me.

It was strong but not unbeatable.

"Get back to safety, " I told Sin in a strained voice.

"No, I can't leave you here to fight them alone," she argued. "You have no idea what you're up against."

"It's my fault they're here. They followed my bond with Juliet, so I'll deal with them."

I heard laughter and spun to find a group of hooded figures standing several feet away from me.

"What makes you think you can stand against us?" one of them asked.

Their proximity made it easier to identify their magic. These were spellcasters.

I didn't know of any demon-hunting spellcasters, especially since no one I knew outside of the Reaper Ridge community believed demons existed.

Since they were spellcasters, I was better trained to fight them, even those using dark magic. The down side was that they were more likely to recognize me as a fugitive.

It seemed best to try reasoning with them first since I was outnumbered.

"I'm not your enemy," I said with my hands up and palms out so they could see I didn't have a magical item to toss their way.

The one who'd first spoken responded. "Then move out of our way and let us kill the demon."

I shook my head. "I can't do that. She hasn't done anything to deserve death." Not that I was aware of, anyway.

"She's a demon," one hissed. "Why defend her?"

"He's trying to keep all her power for himself," another accused. "Stand down and let us take her, or you'll die, too."

It was clear I wouldn't be able to negotiate with them, but I needed to keep them talking longer.

"You think I'll let you have my demon?" I asked with a laugh, pleased when that question led to a very boring speech about how weak I was. That gave me time to focus on the magic flowing around me.

All magical creatures draw their power from natural sources. In most cases, they take energy from the Earth or living things—either plants or animals. This magic had the dark taint of blood magic, possibly even death magic.

The energy from these spellcasters felt so dark that I wanted to recoil, but I forced myself to continue focusing on it.

Once the long rant about how I was messing with powers I didn't understand ended, I spoke again. "Death magic is forbidden among spellcasters."

None of the hooded figures responded at first, likely shocked that I'd figured out their power source so quickly. In truth, I was guessing that it was death magic rather than nonlethal blood magic, but they didn't deny my suspicions.

"I know who you are." I could practically hear the smirk in the warlock's voice. "I don't know why I'm surprised to find one of our biggest traitors among the demons. This is a good day for us. We'll bring you in and drain the energy of that disgusting creature with you."

"Disgusting creature?" Sin asked with a laugh. "Is that the best insult you can come up with?"

I heard the pain and unease in her voice, though I doubted the other spellcasters had. Sin was afraid, but she still hadn't run. It was clear she had no intention of leaving me alone with the demon hunters.

I had trouble holding back my triumphant smile when I found a weak spot in the dark magic. It wasn't much, but it would be enough to send a blast of magic through. That would give us time to escape farther into the protected area.

My power slowly inched through the black magic, picking up speed as it created a bigger hole. As my energy gained momentum, I hoped none of them caught on to what I was doing.

They didn't, and it was almost too late for them to stop me.

The thing about powerful spellcasters is that they're often overconfident. I'd been taught from an early age that it didn't matter how powerful you were; someone could always take you down.

"If you hand over the demon, Dante Verdugo, we may be able to put in a good word for you and save your life," a witch called out. "You'll die a painful death if you defend this creature. We need her power."

"Aren't we already stealing enough power from shapeshifters?" I asked in a bored tone as I continued to focus on working my magic through theirs. I was almost there. It picked up speed the closer it got to the surface.

One of the warlocks laughed. "This situation is too funny. You Verdugos always believed you were better than the rest of us. It's been fun watching the fall of your family. Your poor stepmother is heartbroken."

"Don't you think it's time to go back and face justice?" a witch asked. "You may not care about how this affects the other Azureans, but surely you can't allow your family to suffer for your stupidity. More than your stupidity, they are suffering for your weakness."

I smiled, knowing they were about to see how wrong they were to consider me weak.

My magic burst free in a near blinding flash of light that sent the demon hunters stumbling back.

With the black magic no longer clouding our surroundings, I could clearly see the path back to safety.

I caught Sin's hand and ran, not breathing a sigh of relief until I felt the veil of the protection spell around us.

When I turned, the demon hunters were on their feet again, looking around for us, but they couldn't see beyond the Black Mist.

"I messed up big time," I muttered.

"Yes, but you redeemed yourself," Sin replied. "I was

impressed with how you handled those demon hunters. I told the other demons you were powerful enough to fight them, but they didn't believe me."

My eyes narrowed. "Was this some kind of test? Did you set this up so I would fight the demon hunters?"

"No, but I might have if I'd expected them to be here," she replied. "I just planned to let you connect with your shapeshifter. Demon hunters have never been spotted in this area. I figured we'd have to go to the other side of Reaper Ridge and travel at least a few miles outside of the protected area before we ran into any."

"You planned to test me against them at some point?" I asked. "You wanted the demon hunters to attack me?"

"Eventually," she admitted with no shame.

"And did you plan to warn me about them? Give me any clue as to what I was up against?" I demanded.

She looked at me as if I was stupid. "Why would I warn you if I wanted to accurately judge how you'd do against them?"

"I don't know," I replied angrily. "Perhaps, so that I wouldn't get killed? I thought you liked me. At the very least, I thought you had a sense of self-preservation. *You* could have been killed."

"I do like you," she insisted. "If I didn't like you, then I would have watched you fight the demon hunters from a safer spot. I stayed in case you needed my help."

Her response didn't make me any less angry.

"Are you mad at me?" she asked.

"Yes, but I'll get over it," I replied.

"Because you like me?" she asked with a smile.

"And because I'm starting to realize it's not fair to expect you to act like a spellcaster," I explained.

"Act like a spellcaster?" Her nose wrinkled in disgust. "Certainly not."

We walked in silence for several minutes before she spoke again. "I'm sorry you couldn't talk to your shapeshifter longer."

I sighed and nodded. "Yeah, I miss her. Is it crazy that

I miss her more after communicating with her?"

She shook her head. "No. Every time your magic connects, the bond between you will grow stronger. I want to taste your energy."

She quickly changed to a dog and raced ahead of me. "Demons are strange."

Chapter Thirteen

Pops was furious.

He'd been lecturing me for more than twenty minutes after having spent ten minutes ranting about my stupidity.

I'd held my tongue the whole time because he was right to be angry. Had I simply heeded the warnings and not gone that far out, the demon hunters wouldn't have found us.

Yes, I was angry that no one had given me any specific warnings about why I should avoid that area, but I bit back all my arguments. I could have pushed harder for an explanation. There was no denying I'd screwed up.

He blew out a frustrated breath and sat at the table before running his fingers through his hair and asking me in a much calmer tone, "What were you thinking? You're smarter than this. At least, I thought you were."

"You're right," I agreed. "My bond with Juliet clouded my judgment, and I kept moving closer to the place where the connection felt stronger. I feel a constant draw to her."

"And just how do you expect to avoid being killed when you leave here if you can't focus on anything other than her?" he demanded. "If you ignore your surroundings, you'll be dead in less than a day."

"I felt more focused once I touched on her magic, so I

don't think that will be a problem."

"You don't think period," he muttered.

"Why didn't anyone warn me about the demon hunters?" I asked. "Sin said she didn't expect any there, but you didn't sound all that surprised by my encounter."

"I'm not shocked, but we've never seen any in that area before," he replied. "I still should have mentioned them since we've run into them at the far end of the valley on the other side of Reaper Ridge. I'm sure they'll focus on the area where they saw you more after your encounter."

"Have they found demons on the other side before?" I asked. "Is that why they keep coming back?"

Pops nodded. "We don't lose many over there because the demons don't often leave the protected area, but you've spent enough time around Sin to know how they are. They sometimes let their curiosity land them in dangerous situations."

"I think Sin was trying to help me," I argued.

He snorted. "That might be part of it, but I wouldn't bet on it being the driving force behind her actions."

Sin growled at him from her spot on the floor.

Pops pointed a finger at her. "You could have both been killed."

She yawned and put her head on her front paws.

"As I said, I should have told you about any potential dangers you could encounter near the perimeter of the protected area," he admitted. "I assumed you'd stay with the others on patrol and that one of them would keep you from making that kind of mistake."

"Sin doesn't let the others get close to me," I explained.

"Annoying demon," Pops grumbled, scowling at Sin when she growled again.

"The demon hunters must know spellcasters are working with the demons," I mused. "Why else would they have followed my connection to Juliet back to me? They would have no way of knowing my identity just from touching on my magic."

"They would if you'd worked closely with them on

spells before," Pops argued.

"It's possible," I agreed. "I don't think I know any of the demon hunters."

"You couldn't even see their faces," he reminded me.

"But I had to touch their magic to break free," I reminded him. "I didn't recognize their magic. It seems more likely they were looking for spellcaster magic in the hopes of finding a demon."

"They could have also touched your magic and realized you have a connection to a demon," he suggested.

"But how?" I asked. "I'm not bound to Sin in any way."

Even as I said the words, I felt a niggling doubt.

"Am I?" I asked.

When I looked over to where Sin had been lying on the floor, she was gone.

Pops shrugged. "I sense something that's not quite spellcaster magic. It could just be the way your shapeshifter's magic is bound to yours, but I'm not sure."

I nodded. "I'll ask Sin. She probably went up to my room."

"Don't be surprised if she avoids answering you. She slunk out of here when we started talking about a possible link to her magic," he stated. "I think we can put this behind us. The demon hunters will search that area for a short time, but they'll eventually assume you moved on."

"Why would they think that?" I asked. "They saw me disappear behind the Black Mist, so they have to know there's something here. This is bad."

He waved off my concerns. "Not as bad as you might think. The spell in the Black Mist causes confusion when outsiders get near it. You can go in and out of the spell because the demons and spellcasters responsible for maintaining it made an exception for you. Others get near it and get turned around."

I nodded. "Do you think it's possible someone set me up and told the demon hunters they could find me here if they patrolled the area?"

Pops's eyes narrowed. "Are you saying we have a

traitor who wanted to lead demon hunters to our community?"

I shook my head. "Not so much a traitor as someone who thinks you'd be safer if I wasn't here."

"That's not possible."

There was enough of a delay before his denial that I suspected he thought I might be right.

"I am a danger to everyone here," I told him. "Harboring an Azurean criminal is risky, and I'm sure not everyone was happy about me being brought here."

"What makes you think you're the only Azurean criminal we're protecting?" he asked.

"How many others are there?"

He shrugged. "Only a few now, but we've had more in the past. Our people have been caught spying or trying to release shapeshifters in the past, so we've had to rescue them."

"I'm surprised I never heard about criminals disappearing," I told him.

"We usually find a way to make it look like they were killed in an escape attempt," he explained. "Your trial was more rushed, so there was no time for the usual planning. Since you aren't one of ours, we also couldn't count on you cooperating."

"I'm not one of yours," I repeated his words and waited for him to acknowledge that key difference.

"There are some who feel that way, but I still doubt any would put us all at risk to get rid of you. Few knew where you'd be today. Those involved with patrolling the perimeter all argued that they could keep us safe with you here," he explained.

I nodded, but I still had my doubts.

"Laranissa has a lot of pull with several members of our community," Pops added. "They don't want to see her hurt."

"I never understood her relationship with my father," I remarked. "He loves her, though he's not always good at showing it. I always assumed she also loved him, but it makes more sense that it was just an assignment."

"I wish that was the case," Pops replied. "She was supposed to work at the disposal area so she could give us an accurate count of how many shapeshifters were dying and how they were killed. She was also to report back with details about the hunters. That's how she met your father."

"I didn't know Laranissa had worked there."

"She wasn't there long," he replied. "I never understood her feelings for your father, but she loves him. At least, she did. I'm not sure how much longer she plans to stay. She's considering leaving after what happened with you."

I nodded. "Her relationship with my father has been tenser these last few years. I've often wondered if there would be a breaking point. They're both so different."

"Yes, they are," he agreed. "I once told her that hunters weren't worth her love. She said I needed to see the warlock, not just the hunter. She admired your father's decision to raise all of his children when their mothers didn't want them."

I felt sadness wash over me at the reminder that my father hadn't always wanted me dead. My mother had never wanted anything to do with me, but my father had tried to be there for me.

He might not have done much to protect Serena from Nicolas, but none of us had. After Serena's arrest, my father had argued for leniency and allowed her to move to our wing of the house when her parents turned their backs on her.

"My father is a complex warlock," I stated.

"One who betrayed you," Pops reminded me.

"Yeah, but he doesn't see it that way. Back to the subject of someone possibly wanting to get rid of me. We can't rule out that possibility. I never would have guessed my father would turn his back on me and push for my speedy execution. You can't assume that circumstances won't change how a person feels. For all we know, someone heard the demon hunters say they were looking for me. We just don't know what might have happened."

"You're right," Pops agreed. "I'll look into it. If someone set you up, they'll be dealt with."

"I need to leave. Whether someone here betrayed me or dumb luck caused my run-in with the demon hunters, they'll be back. After this encounter, there are going to be fewer spellcasters and demons who want me here."

"Tell me everything you can about the demon hunters," he prompted. "If you're going to leave, then we'll need to make sure you're better prepared in case you run across them again."

"I believe they're using death magic. It may be a nonlethal type of blood magic, but it felt dark and powerful. They're Azureans."

"Azureans? Are you sure?"

"Almost positive," I replied. "This means other Azureans will come looking for me. Hunters may be sent out here if they think I've met up with Juliet and the rebel shapeshifters hiding her."

"Something tells me the demon hunters aren't going to let many in Azuredale know they saw you," he remarked. "If they captured you, they would have brought you back dead to avoid having you reveal anything about them. They won't want anyone knowing they were out using dark magic to hunt demons. I think they'll do anything to keep their hunting territory a secret."

He had a good point.

"You're probably right. We just have to worry about the demon hunters."

"We'll keep our people from traveling past the Black Mist until the demon hunters give up on finding you or another demon. If they make no progress, they'll move on."

"I'm sorry about this mess. You were safe until I came here."

Pops let out a bark of laughter. "Safe? What makes you think we were safe? We engage in a lot of dangerous activities, and we all know the risks."

"I still feel bad."

"You should, but we need to do something more productive than place blame," Pops stated. "I need to discuss this with the others on the leadership council so we can come up with a plan to deal with the demon hunters, and I'll also bring up your suggestion that we may have a traitor, though I think that's unlikely. While I'm gone, maybe you and your demon can come up with a good plan."

After he left, Sin trotted into the room.

"I don't suppose you want to change to your human form, so we can discuss how I'm going to get to Juliet, do you?"

She cocked her head to the side and stared at me.

"Fine," I replied as I headed up to my room. "I'll plan without you."

It was time to find Juliet.

Chapter Fourteen

I spent several hours trying to figure out the best way to leave without running into demon hunters. I'd had to wait for Pops to return to ask for maps since I wasn't all that familiar with the area close to Reaper Ridge.

After he got the maps for me, I told him I was leaving the next morning, and the fight started.

"Are you trying to get yourself killed?" he roared.

"I told you I was leaving," I reminded him.

"Leaving tomorrow would be suicide," Pops told me as he paced the room. "We need more time to plan, or you'll end up dead or captured, and then all we did to rescue you will be a complete waste."

"I'm grateful for your help," I replied. "If it weren't for you, I'd already be dead. My gratitude to you is part of the reason I'm eager to leave soon. I've put your people in even more danger. What did the others on your council say when they heard about the attack?"

He looked away and didn't respond.

"They want me out. They want me to leave now."

He nodded. "Yes, most want you to leave now. I got you another week here, but some aren't happy about it. I convinced them that giving you more time to plan and train will make it safer for us."

"Do you really think that, or are you just doing what you think Laranissa would want?"

"I'm not looking forward to Laranissa's reaction when she hears I let you leave," he admitted. "She'll be even angrier if I let you go without any preparation, and I'm not sure she'll forgive me if they bring your body back to Azuredale."

"I don't want her angry with you," I assured him. "She knows me well enough that she'll believe you when you tell her I insisted on leaving tomorrow."

"My daughter isn't the only reason I want you to wait," he told me. "Give us a week to get you prepared. You can't help your shapeshifter if you get killed."

"I won't be alone," I replied. "Sin wants to go with me."

"Why?" He sounded shocked. "Are you sleeping with her?"

I laughed and shook my head. "No, it's nothing like that. Well, I suppose she does end up on my bed some nights, but it's just to sleep. She likes me, and she's bored."

"This is unexpected," he mused. "I need to meet with the leadership council again. They'll want to know that a demon has decided to travel with you, especially since she's one of our original demons. I highly recommend you stay in the house until I get back."

"Am I in danger here?" I asked. "Are people angry because of what happened today?"

"They're skittish and worried that you might have drawn more attention to us," he explained. "It would just be better if you stay out of sight until we have a better plan. Is there anything else I should know?"

"Nothing I can think of," I replied.

"Are you going to agree to stay the extra week?" he asked.

I nodded. "Yes, I'll stay one more week. You're right about it being smart to train and plan more."

"You aren't as foolish as I was beginning to suspect," he replied before heading out the front door again.

A week. I could wait one more week.

Chapter Fifteen

Waiting a week to leave wasn't easy.

Each day, the pull of my connection to Juliet grew stronger. I longed to be close to her, even if it was just telepathically.

Though I wanted to ask Sin to arrange another dream meeting, I'd decided it was best if I didn't after our encounter with the demon hunters. Any magic reaching outside of the area could be another beacon for them. I refused to risk the safety of those who'd helped me any more than I already had.

My impatience might have been harder to deal with had I not been so busy getting ready. We spent several hours mapping out the long path I'd take to get to Juliet. I didn't know exactly where she was, so mostly I was trying to get close to where I'd been captured.

Since there were no vehicles to spare, I'd be traveling on foot. It would take me at least three days, and that was assuming I didn't run into any problems that forced me to detour. We'd had to put all of the maps on paper since they couldn't risk me being caught with one of their electronic devices.

The rest of my days were spent training. As a hunter, I was a pretty good fighter, but I learned a few new tricks from the witch in charge of security.

My encounter with the demon hunters had been my first with any spellcaster using death magic. I'd learned a few defensive spells against death and blood magic in Azuredale, so I wasn't completely helpless. Since the demon hunters were from Azuredale, they were likely better prepared to defend themselves against Azurean spells.

I trained with two different spellcasters on various spells that worked against death magic. They'd also taught me a few other defensive spells and one that could temporarily cloak my magic. The last would come in handy when I needed to contact Juliet.

I'd still have to limit my telepathic communication in areas where I might encounter demon hunters. Thankfully, my maps also showed the places they'd been spotted.

It was finally time, and I felt surprisingly sad leaving Pops behind, even if I was also anxious to head out.

I had a pack with the necessities slung over my shoulder. Sin was on my left side in dog form while Pops was on my right as we walked toward the north end of the protected area, a spot where demon hunters had never been spotted. The terrain was rougher at that end, making my journey harder initially, but everyone agreed it was safest.

"This is the stupidest thing any member of my family has ever done," Pops grumbled.

I grinned as I looked over at him.

"Why do you look so happy?" he snapped. "You're about to get yourself killed for some female you barely know. Forget I asked. Your mind is addled."

I laughed and shook my head. "I'm glad you think of me as family. Laranissa has always been a mother to me, and it's nice knowing I have more family, especially when nearly every Verdugo has written me off as a traitor."

"Not the ones who matter. I never much cared for your father. My daughter thinks he may come around and support you eventually, but I don't know if I believe that."

"I'm amazed you were able to get her into Azuredale without arousing any suspicion," I mused. "All it would have taken was one person to question Laranissa's origins."

"That part's easy," he replied. "Laranissa grew up with her mother away from here. She has roots outside of this settlement, like other spellcasters associated with us."

"I heard you refer to her mother as your witch, but you aren't together?"

"I've always considered Laranissa's mother my witch, but she never felt the same connection to me. Our magic isn't compatible. I'm just a romantic fool."

"You? A romantic fool?"

He glared at me. "A warlock doesn't get this irritable without some heartbreak in his past. It's part of the reason I'm so against you putting your life at risk for this shapeshifter. You're young."

"But my situation is different," I argued. "My magic is already partially bound to Juliet's."

"She's not a witch," he stated.

"I know, and it shouldn't be possible based on everything I've ever been taught."

"Have you considered the possibility that this isn't your magic joining? This could be some connection like the familiar bond. For all you know, she could find a shapeshifter mate. What happens then?"

"Even if it weren't for Juliet, I can't abandon Serena," I pointed out.

He nodded. "What are your plans for Serena? You may find a way to get Juliet back to her home, but I doubt they'll offer sanctuary to you and Serena."

"That may not be possible since I've heard the protection spell around the Heathergate Refuge will only allow shapeshifters to enter," I admitted. "For now, the plan is to get Juliet to the Heathergate Refuge. The rebels may be willing to offer me sanctuary."

These were all things I'd discussed with various members of the leadership council already, but Pops had avoided talking about me leaving in the last week. It seemed he'd saved all his questions for our last few minutes together.

He snorted. "So, you have no solid plan, and yet you'll risk it all when this shapeshifter may leave you."

"I've seen you talking to her picture, the one I assume is of Laranissa's mother."

Pops stopped walking and glared at me. "You've been spying on me in the middle of the night?"

"Not intentionally," I replied. "What would you do if your witch was in danger today? Even knowing she doesn't consider you her warlock, could you let her die?"

He let out a frustrated breath but didn't answer my question before he started walking again. "I'm going to be furious if you get yourself killed."

We both stop walking when we reached the very end of the protected area. This was where we had to say our goodbyes. When I hugged him, Pops hesitated for a heartbeat before hugging me back.

"Take care, son." He looked over at Sin. "Don't let anything happen to him, demon, or I'm going to be very angry with you as well."

She looked up at me, putting her paws on my shins. She was in the form of a much smaller black dog, probably no heavier than ten pounds.

"What is it?" I asked.

Pops chuckled. "She wants you to pick her up. It's why she picked a smaller form this time."

"I'm not going to carry you around," I insisted.

She remained where she was, paws on my shins.

"I don't think you're gonna get moving until you pick her up," Pops stated.

"I can always walk around her," I reminded him as I scooped up the irritating demon. "Don't think I'm going to carry you the entire trip," I told her as I stepped out from behind the veil of magic.

I immediately felt my connection to Juliet and sighed in relief.

Soon, I'd be able to hold her in my arms again.

Chapter Sixteen

Juliet

Two days earlier

I'd been snapping at nearly everyone since my brief connection with Dante. Our separation had become even harder since learning he was coming.

For weeks, I'd dreamt of him.

He consumed my thoughts, driving out any plans to return to the Heathergate Refuge. It's not that I'd given up on the idea of going home and dealing with my stepmother, but how could I focus on that when I felt as if a piece of my soul had been ripped away from me?

Communicating telepathically while in human form was all new to me. Alaric was the only one other than Dante I'd done that with, and he'd been a wolf at the time. It also hadn't felt the same as the link I shared with Dante, leaving me with questions and no one to ask.

Would it only work when he was close by?

Had it just been a temporary telepathic link?

I had other questions, but those were the ones that plagued me most. Dante was far from me, yet I'd been able to communicate with him again for a short time.

The relief I felt at knowing he was still alive had brought tears to my eyes. That had been nearly a week ago, and I'd felt nothing since the dark magic had invaded our link.

Every attempt to contact him again was met with a void.

No telepathic communication.

No proof Dante was okay.

I craved the connection to him even more after that brief exchange.

That's how I found myself sitting as far from the rebel shapeshifter settlement as I could get without angering Alaric. He hadn't been amused the day I'd ventured too far in cat form, not that I blamed him. He didn't want me to bring any danger to their community.

"It won't do you any good to sit around and worry about Dante," Serena stated as she approached me. Her hair was loose, with black curls falling around her face as she regarded me with silvery-blue eyes that were just like Dante's.

"I'm not sure there's anything that will do me any good," I grumbled.

"Try looking on the bright side," she suggested.

"Bright side? What bright side?" I asked.

"Dante is still alive," she replied.

"We don't know that. He was in danger when he shut down our link again, so there's no telling if he's still alive. The magic that touched our connection was darker than anything I've ever felt."

"You need to knock it off, Juliet. I get that you're worried. I'm worried, but it won't do you any good to sit around all day trying to connect with Dante. Were you even trying the last time?"

"No," I admitted.

"Then there's no reason for you to keep trying," she stated. "It will happen. Something kept him from reaching out to you before that day, and it must be preventing him again."

I heard footsteps, so I simply nodded. My telepathic conversation with Dante wasn't something I wanted to discuss with others. Most of the rebels already didn't trust me.

"What are you two talking about?" Alaric asked as he approached us.

He had on just a pair of shorts, leaving his torso bare. His light-brown hair was messy, as usual, and his gray eyes were fixed on Serena.

Alaric knew about my last communication with Dante because it hadn't felt right keeping information about the dark magic that had touched my bond from the rebels. He'd decided it wasn't a threat and told me to keep the information to myself. Some shapeshifters still didn't trust us.

He always tried to pretend he was just checking on us or had inadvertently run into us, but I knew the truth; he simply wanted to be around Serena. When we'd first arrived, he'd followed her around, claiming to be worried about her fear of shapeshifters.

Serena had quickly gotten over her fear by spending time around the children. They all gravitated toward her because she was so willing to share spellcaster stories. She was naturally nurturing, and after overcoming her fears, most of the adults no longer intimidated her.

A few still intimidated me.

"Are you listening to us, Juliet?" Serena asked as she waved a hand in front of my face.

I shook my head. "Sorry. My mind wandered. What were you saying?"

"I was reminding you that Dante is a survivor," Serena replied. "We both need to have faith that he can get himself out of whatever mess he's in. There's nothing else you can do."

"Do you think I'll ever see him again?" I asked. "Don't lie to me and tell me what you think I want to hear."

"Probably not," Alaric replied.

Serena scowled and swatted his chest with the back of

her hand. "Why would you say something like that while she's already worried?"

"Because it's the truth," he replied. "She said she wanted the truth. It's always possible he just retreated behind whatever wall of magic he's been hiding behind."

"That makes sense," Serena agreed with a nod. "Dante is smart and cautious. He normally is, anyway. I'll admit he's behaved a bit recklessly where you're concerned, Juliet. If something dark touched your bond, he wouldn't be willing to risk leading the danger to you."

"I suppose." I wasn't convinced, but that explanation gave me some comfort. "He wouldn't risk my life to contact me."

"Do you believe that, or are you trying to make yourself feel better?" Alaric asked.

"I don't know what to think," I admitted. "There's this part of me that feels like I'd know if he died. It doesn't make sense that I feel this way."

"Nothing about your bond makes sense," Serena added.

"Do you think that veil of magic he's hiding behind is the same kind of spell they have around the Heathergate Refuge?" Alaric asked.

"It can't be exactly the same," I replied. "The spells that protect my home are designed to only allow shapeshifters to pass."

"Both spells probably require multiple layers of magic cast by different spellcasters," Serena added. "These types of protection spells are complex and designed to prevent one spellcaster from betraying the others."

"That makes sense," I agreed.

"I don't know how you can feel safe at the Heathergate Refuge," Alaric began. "Spellcasters cast those spells, and you can't trust that one of them won't betray you. They have no honor."

I resisted the urge to smack him. Alaric might have developed a fondness for Serena, but he'd yet to learn how to keep his mouth shut regarding his feelings about spellcasters in general.

"Could you try to avoid sounding like such a jerk?" I asked.

Alaric opened his mouth to argue before looking at Serena and flashing her a sheepish smile. "Present company always excluded when I say something like that. How do you know the spellcasters who make the bracelets won't find a way to make some that allow spellcasters to enter your land without permission?"

"That seems unlikely," Serena argued.

"Why is that?" Alaric asked.

"They don't want us to enter the protected areas," Serena explained.

"That's what they say," Alaric told her.

"If you tell me spellcasters have no honor so you can't trust them, I'll kick you," she warned.

"I met one of the spellcasters who makes the bracelets," I told Alaric. "If the others are anything like Torrent, then I doubt they'd try to help other spellcasters get past the barrier. Torrent knew what I was right away, and he tried to help me."

"Maybe he was lying about helping you," Alaric suggested. "He may have planned to turn you in. He could be the one who tipped off your warlock's brother."

I shook my head. "Torrent could have turned me in the day I met him. Instead, he kept my secret. I trust him."

"The Wylders aren't like other Azurean families," Serena added. "Unlike the Verdugos, they could have familiars, but not a single member of their family has ever had one to the best of my knowledge. I've always gotten the impression they don't support the practice, though they've never spoken out against it. There are rumors that some members of their family went off to live in the woods, preferring a more natural life. I wonder if we could find them and get you a new bracelet, Juliet."

"I've come across the spellcasters living deep within the woods before," Alaric remarked. "Do you really think they can make those bracelets?"

"It's possible," I replied. "Some rumors are just that, while others have more basis in truth."

"I've even heard rumors of the spellcasters deep in the woods being the descendants of those who cast the original spells on the Heathergate Refuge," Serena remarked.

"Interesting," I mused. "I wonder if they can help me get you and Dante past the Ivorfalls as well."

Both were silent for several heartbeats.

"You expect Serena to live among the shapeshifters at the Heathergate Refuge?" Alaric sounded aghast at the idea.

"It's safer for her there," I argued.

"I don't think so," he scoffed.

"Why?" Serena asked.

"Because I can't protect you there," he replied.

"You don't know how long they'll let either of us stay here," I reminded him. "There are plenty here who still aren't all that happy with our presence. What happens when we're told to leave?"

"That won't happen," Alaric insisted. "You can't go back to the Heathergate Refuge. You have to know that. There's no proof these spellcasters in the woods can even help you. It's just a story. Going to look for them would put you at great risk."

"I'm not sure you'd be safe at your old home," Serena added. "Look what they've already done to you?"

"It's probably too late to save your father," Alaric said with no emotion. "If your stepmother is determined to rule, she must have had plans to kill him. He's very likely already dead."

Serena looked furious as she glared at him. "What a horrible thing to say. Juliet already has enough to worry about. Why would you tell her that her father is dead?"

I understood Alaric's reasons, and I knew he might be right. There was always a chance my stepmother would simply wait until my father handed over the power to my stepbrother. That would be the easiest way to avoid conflict at the Heathergate Refuge, but she might not be as concerned with conflict if she had enough shapeshifters backing her. These were all things I'd considered over the last few weeks.

I put a hand on Serena's arm. "It's okay. I've been coming to terms with the fact that my father may be dead. This is about more than my father—it's about my people. I am meant to be their leader, but Alaric is right about you. I think it will be safer for you at the Heathergate Refuge, but it might be risky going to find the Spellcasters who can help with the bracelets. Perhaps I should do this alone."

She snorted. "Don't start with that. I'm not helpless. What about Dante? How will he find you if you're off looking for these spellcasters?"

"I plan to find Dante first," I assured her. "After that, I'm going to do whatever it takes to become the leader my father said I was born to be."

"It's safer for you here," Alaric said with an exasperated sigh. "Leaving is risky and foolish."

"This isn't where I belong," I told him. "If my people won't allow me to return with Dante, then I'll leave, but not before I make sure my stepmother can't cause any more problems."

"And what about your stepbrother?" Serena asked. "You hardly ever talk about him."

"Ellis is still a child." I felt sadness wash over me. "We don't know each other as well as we should, considering we've lived together since his birth. Part of it has to do with the eight-year age gap, but there's also the fact that my stepmother coddled him and kept him away from me whenever possible. I can't imagine he knows what his mother's done."

"If you aren't close to him, then you have no way of knowing he doesn't want you dead," Alaric pointed out.

"I hate to say it, but Alaric is right," Serena added. "I have no doubt Nicolas would have killed Dante if that's what it took to get ahead."

"Ellis isn't like Nicolas," I insisted. "He's not cruel. I just know my brother isn't involved with any of this. We may never be close, but he doesn't want me dead."

"I hope you're right," Serena whispered. "What are you going to do if you can't bring Dante or me back with you to the Heathergate Refuge?"

"I don't know yet," I admitted. "Maybe Dante will have some ideas."

"You need to accept that you may never see Dante again," Alaric stated.

I shook my head. "No, I won't give up on Dante. He's not dead, and we will be together."

Chapter Seventeen

Over the next couple of days, I tried to gather information about the mysterious spellcasters in the woods.

If nothing else, it kept me from spending all day obsessing over Dante. I wasn't sure how much of what I'd been told I could believe. Some shapeshifters claimed to have seen them and gotten close enough to listen in on conversations, but no one could tell me with any certainty if they would be able to help me.

Some of the stories I'd heard sounded too farfetched to be true, especially the talk of alliances with demons. That had come from two older shapeshifters we'd just left.

"Do you think they made all of that stuff up?" I asked Serena. "No one else mentioned anything about demons."

Serena looked thoughtful. "What they said would explain a lot."

"It would?" I asked.

She nodded. "The spells used on the bracelets are strange, and we've always suspected there was some other type of magic involved, but no one could identify it. The family who makes them is very secretive about their methods."

"But that doesn't mean demons are involved," I

pointed out.

"True," she agreed. "Not a lot of Azureans believe in the existence of demons. It could be another type of magic, or it could just be some spellcaster magic other families aren't familiar with."

"How about you?" I asked. "Do you believe in demons?"

She nodded. "Yes, I do. I got lost when I was very young. A witch found me, and she had a dog with her that she claimed was a demon."

"And you believed her?" I asked.

"I know it wasn't a dog," she explained. "There was something about the power emanating from this creature. Of course, I was a child, so no one believed me."

"Was the witch an Azurean?"

"I don't think so," she replied. "I never saw her again. I'd better go. The children want me to play hide and seek with them today."

"All right," I agreed. "I'm supposed to help Alaric gather firewood. He's probably wondering where I am."

She waved as she took off to where a group of children was gathered.

It didn't take me long to find Alaric carrying a large load of firewood.

"Let me take some of that," I offered.

He scowled. "Where were you? You said you'd meet me about half an hour ago. I went by your cabin, but you were nowhere to be found."

"I stopped to talk to some of your older residents about the spellcasters in the woods, and they had a lot to say," I explained. "We kept trying to leave, but they just had more stories to tell."

"Who did you visit?" he asked.

"Hazel and Saxon," I replied.

He laughed. "Yeah, they'll talk your ear off if you let them. Okay, I can see why you're late."

"Have you ever met a demon?" I asked.

"Maybe."

"That's not much of an answer," I complained.

He shrugged. "It's the truth. I'm not sure I'd recognize a demon if I saw one. That is assuming demons are real."

"Hazel and Saxon believe in them," I told him.

"They love to tell stories, so I wouldn't trust everything they say," he argued.

"Serena thinks she met one when she was a child," I added.

He snorted. "I get the impression Serena believes a lot of silly bedtime stories."

I frowned. "Stop treating Serena like a child who doesn't know what she's talking about."

He looked taken aback. "Since when do I treat her like a child?"

"You don't do it so much when she's around," I replied. "It's when you're away from her that your feelings come out."

"What makes you think I see Serena as a child?" he demanded angrily.

I snorted.

"I don't think of her as a child," he argued. "Though she does have an innocence the rest of us lack."

"Hah! That goes to show how blind you are when it comes to Serena. She is far from innocent after all she's suffered. She's a fighter and a survivor. I made the mistake of underestimating her when we first met, but I wouldn't be alive today if it weren't for her."

"I know she's a fighter and a survivor," he replied quietly as he looked away from me.

That's when I realized why he was so determined to view her as a child. Alaric was doing his best to avoid acting on his attraction to Serena.

"You're an idiot if you think that by convincing yourself she's a child or that she's some kind of victim in need of protection, you'll be able to keep your feelings for her in check. You need to stop lying to yourself," I told him.

"How am I lying to myself?" he demanded. "I don't think of Serena as a child, despite what you seem to believe. That doesn't change the fact that she *is* fragile in a lot of ways. Serena needs my protection more than anything else."

I shook my head. "No, she doesn't. You're trying to keep your emotional distance, and we both know it. I'm not judging you since I was in your position with Dante. I was afraid to get closer at first. Now, I regret not taking advantage of my time with him from day one. He is the other half of my soul."

He snorted. "A warlock? Do you truly believe that?"

"Yes, why wouldn't I?"

"Because you're a shapeshifter, and he's a warlock," he replied with an exasperated huff. "It's unnatural."

So much for trying to coax him into accepting his feelings for Serena.

What a jerk!

"I see." My tone was clipped.

"What do you see?" he asked.

"You still see Serena as an enemy like all other spellcasters," I accused. "You're embarrassed to feel anything for her because you think it will cause your people to think less of you."

"That's ridiculous! I never said anything of the sort."

"You don't have to say anything." Serena emerged from the trees. A sad smile played on her lips.

"Serena," Alaric began in a ragged voice.

She shook her head, her smile becoming more forced. "It's okay, Alaric. I know all about the hatred between our kind. You don't need to explain anything to me."

"Serena, I don't want to hurt you," he insisted.

"You haven't," she lied. "Since I got here, you've been very kind. I thought you might have had a change of heart about spellcasters, but I was mistaken. Now, if you'll excuse me, I'm playing hide and seek with some children. They're doing a very good job of hiding this time." Her smile was more genuine when she talked about the game.

"Can we talk, Serena?" Alaric asked as he took a step toward her.

Serena stepped farther away. "I have to go."

She turned and raced off into the trees.

When Alaric moved to follow her, I caught his arm.

"I need to make sure she's okay," he practically growled.

He seemed to blame me for Serena being upset.

"You're the last person she wants to talk to," I told him. "She's embarrassed and hurt. Unless you plan to go after her and tell her you want to be more than her protector, you'll only make things worse for her. Let me handle this."

I had a sliver of hope he'd insist on going after her so he could tell her it didn't matter that she was a witch. It was a silly romantic notion that I blamed on Dante. I'd never been the romantic type before meeting him.

He nodded. "Yes, you should go after her."

"You are such a moron," I grumbled before I hurried after Serena.

Catching up with her was easy since she hadn't gone far.

I sat beside her as we both leaned against the large redwood tree. "He's an idiot."

She turned toward me with a shaky smile. "He's no different from everyone else. The hatred between shapeshifters and spellcasters has existed for hundreds of years. Not everyone can be as lucky as you are with Dante." Her cheeks heated. "I meant lucky that he was willing to risk his life for you after only knowing you a short time. That came out sounding wrong."

"I understood what you meant, and something tells me Alaric would do the same for you," I stated.

"You may be right," she agreed. "I'd risk more than my life for him. I'd risk my heart. That's the biggest difference between him and me, isn't it? Alaric will never give his heart to a witch."

"Would you be as willing to risk your heart if you were still in Azuredale? Could you take that leap with your family watching?"

It was a harsh question, and I didn't know why I was bothering to defend Alaric.

"Sorry," I whispered. "That wasn't fair."

She waved off my apology. "It's okay. You're right to make me think about it from Alaric's perspective."

"No, I've changed my mind," I replied. "I don't want you to feel bad for him. He's a jerk, and you should be mad at him."

Her laugh was weak, but I still counted it as a victory. "He may be a jerk, but I still like him. His situation is very different from mine. My family already considered me an outcast. I'm not sure they would have thought less of me."

"Alaric isn't worth your time."

Her smile was sad. "You're right. I'm not going to waste my time fantasizing about something that won't happen."

"You'll find a male worthy of you," I told her. "You are one of the most amazing people I've ever met, and you deserve someone who is just as amazing. If Alaric can't move past his issues, he isn't good enough for you."

"Thank you, but I'm fine with never finding someone," she insisted. "I resigned myself to being alone because everyone thought I was too strange in Azuredale. Why should I think they would consider me any less strange here?"

I patted her arm. "You aren't strange. You're unique and beautiful. So, are you still playing hide and seek?"

Her eyes widened, and she jumped to her feet. "I need to find the children."

I laughed as I stood. "How about if I help you?"

"Aren't you supposed to be helping Alaric?" she asked.

"Screw Alaric," I replied. "He can handle the firewood alone. Let's go find those children."

Chapter Eighteen

We hadn't gone far when the screams of children alerted us to trouble.

Serena didn't wait for me to react before racing ahead to help them. Those who had believed her a coward were fools.

I ran after her, terrified of what we'd find. The cries for help and blood-curdling screams sent chills down my spine.

Nothing could have prepared me for what we saw as we made it to the clearing where the children often played. Three hairless creatures with slick black skin and long sharp teeth were attacking. One held the lifeless body of a tiny child.

I froze as I took in the horror of the scene.

Serena let out an angry screech and sent a blast of magic that knocked the creature holding the child to the ground before turning her attention to one chasing a child into the woods.

I shook myself out of my shocked stupor and focused on the threat. One monster had a child grasped in its claw-like hands. The child screamed in pain as blood ran down his side.

"Hey!" I shouted, not sure the creature could

understand my language but hoping to get its attention away from the child. "You spineless worm! Look at me!"

The creature dropped the child and turned toward me as another shapeshifter arrived to join the fight.

"Get the children out of here!" I shouted at her.

It would have been nice to have another fighter since I had no clue what I was up against, but someone needed to get the children out of the area. They were in the greatest danger, and they were also a distraction.

"You are not going to hurt any more of these children."

"You think you protect food? We stronger. You no match us. Go back home. Let us eat."

This wasn't the monster's first language, but it could speak and understand it well enough.

I caught the creature off guard with a roundhouse kick that knocked it back. Drawing the knife Alaric had given me to walk patrol with him earlier that week, I lunged and tried to stab the monster's heart—or what I thought to be its heart. That was always a problem when dealing with an unknown species; I had no way of knowing how to kill it.

When I pulled the blade out, it was covered with a sticky black substance that started to solidify around the blade. The monster lunged clumsily at me, probably hoping to rely on its strength to take me down. This time, I stabbed its right eye.

The creature howled as it swiped at me. I made the mistake of trying to pull my knife out before jumping back, and its claws raked across my belly. The scratch burned like fire, and I barely remained on my feet.

Luckily, the creature seemed too distracted with the knife in its eye to attack me again. It continued to scream as it tried to get its claws around the hilt. It couldn't make a fist small enough to grasp it.

I looked around and saw that the creature Serena had knocked back with her magic was on its feet again. The shapeshifter was trying to fight him off while carrying an injured child. She was at a disadvantage with a child in one arm. She'd been able to keep the creature from going after the others, but she needed help if she was going to get away with the injured child.

I threw a rock at the monster, catching him on the side of the head. I hoped to get him to look my way so I could toss another stone at his eye since going for an eye seemed effective.

All I needed to do was give the children time to get out of the area and wait for the other shapeshifters to arrive to help us. Serena might also be back soon. At least, I hoped she was okay.

I tossed two more rocks but missed both times. The burning pain from my injury, combined with blood loss, were affecting my aim. I began backing away, needing to grab more rocks.

The monster's burst of speed caught me off guard as he rushed me and tackled me to the ground.

It was much stronger, but I still managed to break free and scramble to my feet. It stood, and I was able to shove it back before it could strike. It lunged again, and I leaped to the side to avoid its claws.

I needed help.

My back-up came in a surprising form.

Suddenly, my link to Dante fully opened again.

First, I sensed his relief at feeling the touch of my mind. That reaction quickly changed when he sensed the danger to me.

I felt his power flow through me. I'm no witch, so I can't cast spells or send bursts of magic out. I don't even know the words to any spells, or so I thought.

"Asna haria fireno!" I shouted with my hands out and my palms pointing toward the creature who was lunging at me again.

Blue flames shot from my hands and slammed into the monster. It screamed and fell back onto the ground, writhing and twitching as the fire consumed it.

Once there was nothing more than a pile of black ash on the ground, I looked at my palms.

"How did you do that?" Serena asked in awe as she

approached me.

I shook my head. "I don't think that was me. I don't even know the meaning of the words that came out of my mouth."

"The magic came from you, and you cast the spell," Alaric stated.

I hadn't noticed him, but when I looked around, several other shapeshifters had also arrived.

"I know it came from me," I snapped before taking a deep breath. "Sorry. This wound is making me irritable. I don't know what happened. I can't cast spells. That's not possible."

"It's one of Dante's spells," Serena remarked as she regarded me with a curious expression. "What made you decide to use that one?"

I shook my head. "I already told you I'm not even sure what I said or why I said it. No, that's not exactly true. My connection to Dante opened, and I simply acted. I know who I can ask."

"Dante? Can you hear me?"

"Yes, and I can't tell you how good it is to have you back in my mind. I've missed you."

"Was that your magic I used?" I asked.

"I suppose it was, though I'm not sure how that's possible," he admitted. *"I was thinking that I knew the perfect spell to deal with those monsters and wishing I could send my magic to you."*

"Well, apparently, you can."

"What was that thing you just killed?" he asked.

"I was hoping you'd know since you were the one to figure out a spell to use against it," I replied. *"Those horrible things came after the children. At least one of them died today."*

"I've never seen anything like that," he told me.

"Where are you? I've been so worried since I lost contact with you. I was afraid you'd been captured or killed."

"Sorry for worrying you. The place I was staying had

powerful magic that made it impossible to contact you," he explained. *"I'm heading your way, but it will take me several days to get there. I'm traveling with a demon, and we need to avoid running into demon hunters or anyone from Azuredale."*

"You're traveling with a demon? Is this demon your friend?"

"Yes, at least, I think she's my friend," he replied.

"Juliet?" Serena called out. She sounded extremely upset, not that I was surprised, considering how close she was to all the children. The loss of any child bothered me, but I knew it hurt her more.

"I have to help Serena," I told Dante. *"This has been upsetting for her."*

"I understand," he assured me. *"Sin, the demon with me, says I need to focus on our surroundings, so it's probably just as well."*

"I miss you so much."

"I miss you, too, Juliet."

I felt a moment of panic as our mental connection went silent before realizing it wasn't like the last time. Dante hadn't disappeared; I still felt him in the back of my mind, and I could reach out to him. That knowledge allowed me to breathe a sigh of relief.

I turned and placed a hand on Serena's shoulder. "Are you okay?"

"No," she admitted, "but I'll be fine. Were you using your telepathic link with Dante?"

I nodded. "Yes. It's probably how I was able to use his magic. He's not completely sure how it worked for us, but he thought of the spell and wished he could send his magic to me right before I used the spell."

"That's not possible," Alaric argued. "A spellcaster can steal energy from a shapeshifter, but they can't give any energy back."

"That can't be true," I insisted. "I'm not a witch, and that was Dante's spell. I've also channeled his magic to activate a healing spell before."

"I can feel remnants of his magic in the air," Serena stated as she looked around. "It's as if he's here with us."

"We'll have to discuss this later." Alaric still didn't seem convinced I'd used Dante's magic.

Serena looked over at the tiny body of the child we'd lost. "He was such a sweet boy. I can't believe he's gone."

Alaric slipped an arm around her shoulders and pulled her close. "Thanks to you and Juliet, the other children survived. This could have been much worse. There is only one other serious injury, but the child should recover. You're amazing."

Serena nodded as she stepped out from under his arm.

"I did what anyone would have done under the circumstances. I suppose it's a good thing you had a spellcaster here since these things seem much harder to kill without magic." Her attention shifted to me. "After we get your wound cleaned and bandaged, can you help me check on the other children? They must be terrified."

I nodded. "Of course. Do you know what these things were, Alaric?"

He shook his head as he looked over at the pile of ash. "I've never seen anything like this. Much as I hope we never see one of these again, that seems unlikely."

I hoped he was wrong. I didn't want to fight another one of those things.

Chapter Nineteen

We didn't get to check on the children until nearly two hours later.

First, we'd had to endure an interrogation from dozens of distraught parents. I didn't blame them for their fears or desire for answers. Unfortunately, we didn't have many answers.

I'd never seen anything like those creatures, but I could tell many parents didn't believe us. It made sense that they'd be suspicious since we were newcomers.

No one had seen the monsters before our arrival, so they naturally wondered if we had something to do with the attack. Most didn't seem to think we had arranged the attack, but there were more than a few who suspected the creatures were drawn to us somehow.

It could have gone much worse. I'd been worried we'd be accused of being in league with the monsters. I already knew that saving others from a threat didn't mean some wouldn't blame me.

Alaric and the shapeshifters who'd arrived with him kept quiet about me channeling Dante's power, though I didn't know why. They also didn't say one word in our defense and left right after our questioning.

By the time we finished talking to the parents, getting

my wound wrapped, and checking on the children, I was exhausted. Serena seemed to be in even worse shape, so we headed back to the cabin.

"This has been one of the worst days of my life." Serena's voice was flat as she collapsed onto her bed in our shared room.

I settled onto my bed with a sigh. "You were amazing out there. You didn't hesitate to help the children."

"What kind of person would hesitate to help them?" She didn't give me a chance to respond. "How did it feel when you used Dante's magic?"

"Natural," I replied as I thought of how it had flowed through me. "Yet strange and a little scary. I guess I didn't feel those things until *after* I used his power."

"This was like when you changed into a large cat," she remarked. "Dante's magic must have had something to do with that as well."

"It must have," I agreed.

I'd only been able to change into a larger cat that one time.

"I wonder if I can do that now that I'm connected with Dante telepathically. Perhaps I can draw on his energy when I need it."

She propped herself up to look at me. "You should try it now."

I shook my head. "No, I've already drawn on his magic today. I don't know if it will take a toll on him and make it harder to defend himself. I'm not going to use any of his power unless it's a life or death situation."

"You're right. I hadn't even considered that this might drain Dante. Did he seem like he's really okay? You don't think he was trying to keep you from worrying, do you?"

"I don't think he was keeping anything from me. He didn't exactly tell me he's safe, just that he's on his way here."

"How does he know where *here* is?" she asked.

"The same way I know I could find him now that our connection is open again," I explained. "If I focus, I can see the threads of his magic. As long as the bond between us is open, I can find him.”

“I’ve never heard of anything like this happening before,” she said thoughtfully. “Even among bonded spellcasters, they can’t track each other using their joined magic. They can’t track using their bond with a familiar either.”

“This is all new territory,” I admitted. “What else do you know about demons?”

“Nothing, really,” she admitted. “I just met the one, though it may not have been a demon. Why do you ask? Do you think those things from earlier were demons?”

“I don’t know what those things were. Dante is with a demon, and he didn’t say those things were demons.”

“Dante is with a demon?” she asked.

“Yes,” I began. “I’m having trouble wrapping my mind around it, too. That and the fact that her name is Sin.”

“Sin seems like an appropriate name for a demon,” she remarked. “I wonder if it’s her real name.”

I shrugged. “It could be a nickname. Are you hungry? I think we still have some leftovers I can heat up.”

“I’m not hungry,” she replied. “Go ahead and eat if you are.”

I shook my head. “I’m fine. It’s too early to go to sleep. What would you like to do?”

“You don’t have to babysit me if you want to try connecting telepathically with Dante again.”

I wanted to talk to Dante again, but I was worried about Serena, and I knew Alaric or one of the others could come for us soon.

“Now’s not the time,” I replied.

“Because of me?” she asked.

“That’s part of it,” I admitted. “You don’t seem like you’re ready to be left alone. Dante may also be too busy. He told me he needed to focus on his surroundings earlier.”

“I think I’m going to take a nap.” She paused before whispering, “I hope I don’t have a bunch of nightmares.”

"I'm sure we'll both have nightmares after today," I replied.

"That poor child didn't deserve to die," she whispered.

"No," I agreed with a sad sigh. "I'm glad we killed those things."

"Me too," she said with a yawn as she laid down and closed her eyes.

I only planned to close my eyes for a few minutes, but it wasn't long until I was sound asleep.

Chapter Twenty

I awoke to someone pounding on the cabin door.

Serena jerked awake in a panic before groaning and covering her eyes with her arm.

We'd both had a restless night, but no one had come to discuss the attack, much to my surprise. It seemed they were ready to talk to us now.

"We're in for another long day," Serena grumbled as she climbed out of bed and finger-combed her long, black curls. "I guess we should be thankful they didn't come to wake us up last night."

"I was just thinking the same. At least we got some sleep." There was more pounding on the door as I got to my feet. "Give me a minute!"

"Do you think they'll send us away after this?" Serena asked nervously.

"Send us away? Why would they do that?" I asked as I went to open the door. "We saved all but one of the children. Had we not been here, they might all be dead. We're heroes."

"You also saved Dante," Serena called out. "That didn't stop Nicolas from making my uncle doubt your motives."

"Yeah, being a hero doesn't mean people will appreciate what you've done. They might send us away," I agreed with my hand on the door. Anyone outside would be able to hear me. "We're planning to leave anyway. It would be nice to have more time to plan, but we may no longer have the luxury of time."

I opened the door to Alaric. His jaw was clenched as he looked past me to Serena.

"You're absolutely right," Serena agreed as she came up beside me and crossed her arms in front of her chest. "It will be inconvenient to bump up our timeline, but we'll figure it out together. I can't see why they'd tell us to leave. We saved those children and deserve thanks. Hopefully, others will see that and possibly even stand up for us."

"Do you honestly think I blame the two of you for what happened?" Alaric demanded.

"We have no way of knowing with the mixed messages you sent yesterday. One minute, you were telling me I'm a hero, and the next, you did nothing to defend me," Serena snapped. "You don't think very highly of spellcasters, so why would I expect you to see the best in me?"

Alaric let out a frustrated breath and ran his fingers through his hair. "Don't make this about our other issues, Serena."

"Your issues with spellcasters are very much a part of this discussion," I answered for Serena. "We want to know if we should start packing."

"The leadership council wants to meet with you," Alaric stated. "Now."

"Are you going to defend us, or have you decided we're responsible for those monsters attacking the children?" Serena demanded.

"I trust you," Alaric insisted. When we both gave him doubtful looks, he continued. "It's true. If I didn't trust you, I would never have brought you back here where you could get my people killed. I spent most of the night fighting with the others, and I'm in no mood to fight with you. Can I come in for a minute so I can tell you what's going on before we go to the meeting?"

I nodded and stepped aside so he could enter.

Serena still looked angry, but I didn't know how much of that was related to worries Alaric didn't trust us and how much had to do with his rejection of her.

Alaric took a seat at the table, leaned back in his chair, closed his eyes, and let out a tired sigh. "This whole situation is such a mess. If I could think of a safe place for you, I would send you away in a heartbeat."

"What did they decide?" Serena asked.

"No decisions have been made yet," he replied. "They want to talk to you first."

"Talk or interrogate?" I asked.

Serena stepped closer to my side, the only sign she gave that she was nervous about his answer.

"A little of both," he admitted. "There are those who back you, so their questions will be less of an interrogation." His attention moved to Serena. "The father of the injured child is very powerful among our leadership council, and he's on your side. Others from our community came forward in your defense after you saved so many of our children. They don't believe you were in league with the monsters."

"But there *are* some who think we're in league with those things that attacked the children?" Serena demanded. "People honestly believe I would have brought those things here to kill that child? How could they think such a horrible thing about me?"

"Few believe that. It's unlikely anyone will be able to convince enough members of the leadership council of that theory for it to go anywhere," Alaric assured her. "I'm mentioning it now because I don't want you to be surprised when we get there. I want you to understand that you have enemies among us now."

I snorted. "We've had enemies since the day we arrived."

Alaric didn't argue; he simply got to his feet and gestured to the door. "We should go now. They're already going to complain about how long it took me to bring you there."

"Fine," Serena replied. "First, we need a few minutes to get ready. I'd rather not face them looking like I just rolled out of bed."

When Serena started toward the bedroom, Alaric caught her hand as she passed him. "I'm sorry about everything that's happened, Serena."

Her lips lifted into a cynical smile. "You're sorry, but it doesn't change how you feel, does it?"

His guilty expression was answer enough. Serena pulled her hand from his and continued toward the door.

I glared at him. "You're a jerk, and you don't deserve her."

"You're right," he agreed quietly. "I don't deserve her."

Chapter Twenty-One

It was uncomfortably quiet when we entered the meeting hall. It was even more unnerving than I'd expected. Still, I reminded myself that I was the princess of my people. I would not cower in fear or show any sign of weakness. I also had to consider Serena. She needed me to remain strong.

Alaric took a seat beside his mother at the front of the room. She didn't look at us—a bad sign. In fact, several members of the council looked away as we stood before them.

A tall shapeshifter stood and walked around the table to approach us. I could practically feel the power radiating from him.

The leader's long black hair went almost to his waist. His skin was a couple of shades darker than mine, and his eyes were pale green.

"Thank you for coming to the aid of our children," he said as he placed a hand on each of our shoulders. His lips lifted into a slight smile.

"We couldn't let them die," Serena replied.

"But there are many who would have," he told her. "A lot of spellcasters wouldn't have considered young shapeshifters worth saving."

"Serena isn't like other spellcasters," Alaric called out.

The shapeshifter looked irritated with Alaric's interruption. "You've already had your say. We need to hear from Juliet and Serena now."

"We need to know what those things were!" a female shouted as she shot to her feet. "You brought them here."

The male talking to us turned toward her. "Sit down. Your theatrics won't help us get any answers." His attention returned to us. "Had you ever seen anything like those creatures before yesterday?"

We both shook our heads, and I replied, "I've never even seen pictures of something like that in stories. I know some species are rarely spotted. I'd only seen a nāga in books until recently, but others had spotted them, so I knew they existed."

"Same here," Serena added. "It seems strange that there could be creatures like this around without anyone having seen them. They were distinctive and aggressive, not something one could miss."

"I agree," the leader stated. "That's one of the reasons some of our community members are suspicious."

"Maybe it was a different variety of shapeshifter," Serena suggested. "That could explain why we've never seen them look this way."

"It still seems unlikely that no one would have ever seen them in this form. Shapeshifters only have two forms," the leader remarked.

"How often do you leave this area?" I asked. "And how far from here do you travel?"

"We have to send people out for supplies regularly," he replied. "They stay fairly close, within a fifty-mile radius."

He might have been exaggerating that radius to avoid giving too much away about their location. I didn't know exactly where we were.

"Do your children leave this area?" Serena asked. "They went after the children, and that may be their usual prey. Our children don't often travel outside of the safety of Azuredale."

"And ours are never allowed past the border of the Ivorfalls," I added. "If these things hunt children, they'll hunt in areas not protected by a spell."

"But you don't know that's the case," he pointed out. "Unless you're lying about not knowing what they are."

"The one that spoke to me accused me of protecting its food," I explained. "They wanted Serena and I to leave, making me think they don't consider us food."

"She's lying!" someone shouted. "She knows they feed on children because she led them here!"

"That's a lie!" Serena shot back. "We would have never let anything happen to your children. I spend a lot of time with them, and it breaks my heart that one was killed. It also breaks my heart that they'll all live with fears they didn't have before yesterday. They've lost a piece of their innocence that they can never get back. I know all too well the toll that takes on a person."

Alaric started to stand, but his mother placed a hand on his arm. He didn't look happy, but he remained seated.

"How do you think we should handle this situation?" the leader asked as he stepped back and regarded us.

I shrugged. "I don't know. It all depends on how much of a threat everyone here thinks we are to your safety. Do you think we led those creatures here?"

"Since I believe you're right about them hunting children, they weren't after you," the leader stated. "I also don't believe you wanted to hurt the children."

"But that doesn't mean you want us to stay," I added.

"We should leave soon, anyway," Serena remarked.

"Absolutely not!" Alaric shouted. "You aren't going anywhere!"

"Alaric!" his mother hissed. "Sit down now!"

He continued to glare at Serena, and for several tense moments, I was certain he wouldn't back down.

"Sit down, please," Serena said quietly. "You're only going to make matters worse for us."

"Leaving is not an option," Alaric said as he sat.

"I'm inclined to agree with Alaric," the leader who'd

been speaking added.

I felt icy fear race up my spine at his words, but I pushed it down to ask, "Are you saying we *can't* leave?"

"Not without permission," he replied.

"What if I request permission to leave today?" I asked.

"It would be denied," he admitted.

"So, we're prisoners," Serena spat out.

He shook his head. "You're not prisoners. Everyone needs permission to leave the protected area."

"But we can't leave because you don't trust us," Serena argued. "That's an entirely different situation. You especially don't trust me because I'm a spellcaster."

I was worried Serena's blatant challenge would anger the leader who'd yet to share his name, but he didn't seem the least bit annoyed with her tone. "There are many among us who don't trust you, and the leadership council has to take their feelings into consideration."

"I understand," I replied as I caught Serena's hand and squeezed it. "Do you have more questions for us?"

He gave me a slight smile. "Oh, yes, I'm just the first to question you."

Chapter Twenty-Two

More than two hours later, we were finally able to leave the meeting. Every time I thought they were about to release us, a new round of questioning started.

Alaric had avoided any further outbursts, but he'd looked like a caged wolf trying to break free the entire time.

When someone was assigned to take us back to the cabin, Alaric stood.

"I'll walk them back."

More than one shapeshifter, including his mother, looked like they wanted to argue, but they all held their tongues.

Once we were away from the meeting hall, Alaric muttered, "You foolish females have a death wish."

Both Serena and I stopped to glare at him.

"Foolish females?" I asked.

"What is your problem?" Serena demanded with her arms crossed in front of her chest.

I put up a hand before Alaric could respond. "Let's do this inside."

He nodded, and we finished walking to the cabin.

Once I shut the door, Serena said, "Answer my question."

"You can't possibly think leaving here is a good idea,"

he stated. "Don't pretend you're not thinking about leaving even sooner now. You have nowhere to go and no protection."

"And you think we're safe here when many of your people believe we're a danger to them?" Serena demanded. "There may not be that many who think we're in league with those monsters, but they believe our presence is a threat."

"She's right," I agreed. "We were never completely safe here, but things have gotten worse. I'm not about to wait around until they decide we can't ever leave."

"I promised to keep you safe, and I will," Alaric insisted angrily. "Who will protect you if you leave? I'm sure you've already been sentenced to death, Serena. There may still be allies among your people, Juliet, but you have no way of knowing who they are."

I'd kept my temper under control for the meeting, but I was tired of accusations and plots against me. I was also tired of seeing Serena hurt by Alaric.

Alaric became the target of all my pent-up anger.

"Stop acting like Serena is helpless. Spellcaster magic protected the children. More children would have died without her, so I think you should have a little more respect for her abilities. You and your people should be thankful there was a witch here when those creatures attacked since spellcaster magic worked against them."

"Her usefulness was discussed before you were summoned to the meeting," he replied softly.

Silence fell over the room for several heartbeats.

"So, you discussed how you can use me?" Serena asked, sounding more hurt than angry. "What did you decide?"

"That we can't let you leave," he admitted without meeting her gaze. "There are still those who want you cast out, but the majority of the leadership feel you should stay to help us deal with any future threats from those monsters."

"Are you saying we can't leave?" I demanded. "We

were told we couldn't leave without permission, but we won't be granted permission to leave under any circumstances, right?"

"It's not that simple," he argued.

"It seems simple to me," Serena snapped. "It's a yes or no question."

"Either we can get permission to leave, or we're prisoners. Which is it?" I pushed.

He looked away, but Serena stalked toward him and smacked his chest hard. "You owe us an honest answer."

"You can't leave."

"So, we're prisoners because your leadership doesn't know if they'll need us again." Serena sounded calm, though I sensed the effort it took to contain her anger. "We aren't welcome here, but we can't leave." Her gaze shifted to the floor, and she clenched her fists.

"Now, you know how my kind feels," Alaric said in a nasty tone.

"That was a completely messed up thing to say," I told him. "You know Serena's sacrificed a lot for shapeshifters. She's given up *everything*."

Serena met Alaric's gaze, and I'd never seen her look quite so cold. "I was attacked by a shapeshifter when I was thirteen. There are scars on my belly and thighs from the attack. I have every reason to think of your kind as dangerous animals, yet I gave up my freedom trying to save a shapeshifter. Most of my family turned on me because they saw my compassion for shapeshifters as a weakness. I carried a knife everywhere I went for years for fear of being attacked by my cousin because he considered my kindness a weakness. I will not be judged by you."

Alaric opened his mouth to speak, but Serena put a hand up to stop him. "Don't you dare talk to me. I thought you and your people were somehow better. You're not, and I regret wasting my time on you, Alaric. You don't deserve my time or my love."

"Serena," he began in a pleading tone.

"Get out!" she shouted. "I wish I still had my knife so I

could stab you in your black heart."

I sensed her angry magic swirling around the room. She wouldn't kill him, but she would hurt him if he didn't leave.

"Get out," I told him.

For several heartbeats, it seemed he was about to argue before he let out a sad sigh and walked out the door.

Serena still had her fists clenched at her sides, and she didn't say a word.

"Is there anything I can do for you?" I asked.

She shook her head. "No, I'll be fine. We need to start planning. It might be a good time to figure out where Dante is."

"You're right," I agreed. "This isn't the safest place for him."

"I don't know if I can leave the children unprotected."

I nodded. "Maybe you can come up with a protection spell."

"That's a good idea," she agreed. "Can you ask Dante if he has any ideas for the spell while I brainstorm? I'm sure we can come up with some sort of deterrent for those monsters."

"All right," I agreed. "You're planning to stay if we can't find a spell to protect the children, aren't you?"

She hesitated. "I don't know. Let's work on this for now."

"I can't leave you here," I told her.

Anger flashed briefly in her eyes. "Don't try controlling my life like Alaric. I'm tired of people controlling my life."

I moved closer and hugged her. "I'm sorry. Whatever you decide, I'll support you."

Chapter Twenty-Three

While I could still sense Dante, I hadn't connected with him telepathically for more than a few brief moments since the meeting. I'd wanted desperately to discuss what had happened, but he'd cut me short. Though I'd been disappointed, I understood that he needed to remain focused on his surroundings.

When I finally heard his voice in my head again, I felt some of the tension gripping me ease.

"We just stopped to get some sleep."

"Are you still safe?" I asked.

"As safe as I can be," he replied. *"My people want me dead, and I'm traveling with a demon who doesn't seem to realize I could be killed much easier than her. She may not care all that much if I die."*

"Isn't she with you because she likes you?" I asked.

"Sometimes, I'm sure she likes me, but other times, I think she only follows me around out of curiosity. I think her opinion of me changes from hour to hour. What's bothering you? I've sensed your unease all day."

"There have been some complications here," I explained before briefly filling him in on what had happened. *"We may need to leave soon, but I'm not sure Serena wants to go."*

"Why would she want to stay after the way they treated her? That shapeshifter should be thankful my cousin feels any fondness for him. He doesn't deserve her."

"On that, we agree. Serena is worried about the children. It's always possible the rebels won't be able to defend them if we leave. I don't know if there are more of those things wandering around. I don't even know what they are. Serena is going to try to add to the protective spell around the area. We were hoping you could help. Did you ask your demon if she's ever seen anything like them?"

"She referred to them as soul eaters and confirmed that they hunt children. Since then, she's remained in dog form, so I haven't gotten any more answers."

"She's a shapeshifter?"

"Yes, demons can change into anything they want," he explained. "They're very powerful. It seems demon magic helped make the original shapeshifters."

"Serena thinks she may have met a demon in dog form. I'd never met anyone who believed demons existed until recently."

"I don't think the demons want others to believe in their existence. Some spellcasters know, but they've kept that information to themselves."

"The demon hunters are spellcasters, right?" I asked.

"Yes," he agreed. "I don't know how they've been able to keep something this big from the other Azureans, but I suppose it doesn't matter. Where are you planning to go when you leave the rebel shapeshifters?"

"There are rumors of spellcasters living in a community away from Azuredale who may be able to help me get a bracelet and perhaps get you and Serena past the Ivorfalls."

"Do you honestly think your people would accept two spellcasters?"

"You saved my life," I reminded him.

"Alaric owes you and Serena his life, but it's only kept you safe there for a short time."

"You're right," I agreed. "I need to go back to make sure my people are safe, but I can't promise they'll instantly accept you. If you don't want to come with me, I won't blame you."

"I'm going with you, but we both need to accept that I may not be able to stay there."

"Where will you go?" I asked. "You can't go back to Azuredale, and I'm not going to let you go anywhere without me."

"What about your people?" he asked.

"I don't know," I replied. "All I know is I'm not going to lose you again. I want to go back and take my place as the future leader, but my father will either have to accept you or start training Ellis."

"I should ask you if you're sure, but I can't stand the thought of being separated from you again," he admitted. "There's a spellcaster community much farther north where they don't keep familiars. Azureans trade with them sometimes, but I've heard they look down on us because of our familiar practice. Serena and I may be able to seek sanctuary there. I think we should go there first to see if they'll accept you as well. If not, we can try farther north."

"So, we'll run from one place to the next, all in the hopes we won't be killed."

"What else can we do?" he asked. "You don't even know if these spellcasters living in the woods will help you. They may turn you over to the Azureans. Any plan we make has its risks."

"You're right. I suppose we don't have much choice. First, we'll try to get the bracelets, and then we'll deal with my people. After that, we can figure out our next move if we can't stay at the Heathergate Refuge. Are you sure you want to go there with me?"

"Do you honestly think I have any choice other than to follow you?" he asked.

"Yes," I replied. "You can always go with Serena and find a safe place for both of you while I take care of my *people. I can meet up with you once I know they're safe."*

"And you think it will be that simple to walk away from you, Juliet? That I can let you walk into danger?"

"I understand how strong the bond is between us, and it will be just as hard if I need to be away from you, but we may have no choice until after I deal with my stepmother. I can't walk away from everything like the Juliet in your play did."

"Do you mean like I did for you?"

Dante had broken every rule to keep me safe. He was now a warlock without a home, one with a death sentence if he ever returned, and it was all because of me.

"It's not the same thing, Dante. You sacrificed your life for me, but I'm talking about sacrificing the lives of others. If it was only about sacrificing my old life in the Heathergate Refuge, I'd do it in a heartbeat to be with you. I love you, but I'll never be able to live with myself if I don't try to help my people and save my father. I have to do this. Please, try to understand."

"I understand," he reluctantly agreed. *"That doesn't mean I'm happy about this. I need to think and try to find a way to keep Serena safe while I help you."*

I felt tears burn the backs of my eyes. *"I love you so much, and I'm glad you want to be my side. Please, don't try telling Serena what she has to do. She's grown much stronger, and she's tired of being coddled. She wants to help me."*

"All right," he agreed. *"I'm used to thinking of her as fragile, so don't get mad at me if I mess up. I need to get some sleep. If I'm reading the magic correctly, I'll reach you no later than the day after tomorrow. That is, assuming we don't run into any problems. I'll see if I can come up with some ideas for the protection spell. Hopefully, I can get some input from Sin."*

"Be careful."

"You too."

Chapter Twenty-Four

Serena was writing down notes for the protection spell when I finished my telepathic conversation with Dante, so I decided to clean our clothes and make dinner.

She only stopped long enough to eat before getting back to work. She ended up falling asleep, surrounded by a pile of notes.

I gathered up all of her notes and moved them to the table so none would get knocked onto the floor before I headed to bed.

Though I was exhausted after the stress of the last couple of days, I still had trouble falling asleep. My mind kept wandering to all the things that could have gone wrong at the Heathergate Refuge and all the dangers Dante faced.

After a long night with little sleep, I was still dragging when we sat down for breakfast.

"How did you sleep?" I asked Serena.

"Great, but I can tell you didn't sleep well," she replied. "Did you get bad news from Dante? I'm sorry I didn't ask yesterday, but I got caught up in my work. It was hard to stop when the ideas were flowing. I figured you'd have interrupted me if Dante had any suggestions for the spell."

"No bad news, and you're right about him not having

anything to add yesterday. He says the things that attacked the children are called soul eaters and that they prey on children. Unfortunately, he didn't have any more information about them. He's going to let me know if he has any ideas for the spell."

"He's never been as good with this type of spell, but that's okay since I may not need his help. What was bothering you last night?"

"Nothing new," I assured her. "The last couple of days have just been extra stressful, and I couldn't get my mind to shut off."

"I could probably whip up a sleep spell for you tonight," she offered.

I considered her offer before shaking my head. "Thank you, but I don't want anything that might make it hard for me to wake up if there's trouble."

"That's part of the reason you aren't sleeping," she remarked. "You're too worried there will be a problem, so you can't get your mind to shut off."

"You're right," I agreed. "Are you trying to convince me to use a sleep spell?"

She shook her head. "No, because that stress will just carry over into your sleep. You do need to try to get more rest. Maybe you can take a nap today."

"Good idea," I agreed. "Dante thinks he found a safe place for you."

I told her about the spellcaster community up north.

It looked like she was at least open to the idea.

"Is that where Dante's been staying?"

"No, but he still seems sure they'll help you," I replied.

"And you?" she asked. "Does this mean you've decided against returning to the Heathergate Refuge?"

"No, I'm still going to try to get back to my people, but it could be dangerous for you."

She looked furious.

"I'm not saying you can't go with me," I quickly added. "In fact, I told Dante he shouldn't try taking the choice away from you. All I'm doing is telling you about all your options."

"Do you honestly think I'd let you, my best friend, face any danger alone?" she asked.

I smiled and shook my head. "No, but I wish you would. I hate the thought of you being hurt."

"I know how you feel," she replied. "That's why I'm going with you, assuming I can leave without putting the children in danger."

"How is your protection spell going?" I asked.

She grinned. "Better than I would have expected. It's been over a year since I've cast any kind of protection spell, but everything I studied is coming back to me. I should be able to weave this into the spells surrounding the area. The children will have to stick closer to their homes, but they'll have a little more freedom with the spell."

"That's good news," I told her. "I'm glad you'll be with me. We make a good team."

"We certainly do," she agreed.

"I won't be mad or hurt if you decide you don't want to go to the Heathergate Refuge," I assured her. "This is my fight."

She waved off my words. "No one gets to have their own fight. You're more family to me than a lot of the people I grew up with. Your fight is my fight. I'll be glad to get away from here."

"Alaric is a fool."

"Who said anything about Alaric?" she asked.

"I know you aren't looking forward to leaving the children," I replied.

She sighed. "I do need to get away from Alaric."

"I wish he would stop judging you based on his hatred of spellcasters."

"That's not the biggest problem with him," she stated. "He thinks I'm weak, just like my family always has. How can he possibly still think that after what happened the other day? He's never seen me cower like I did in Azuredale, yet he still thinks I'm some silly witch who can't take care of herself."

"I don't think that's it," I remarked. "At first, I did, but now, I think he's afraid."

"Of what?" she asked.

"Losing you."

"But he doesn't have me," she argued. "He doesn't *want* to have me."

"Or he doesn't think he *can* have you," I suggested. "I'm not trying to excuse his behavior, and I still think he doesn't deserve you, but his reasoning is more complex than we often give him credit for."

She nodded and let out a tired breath before responding. "It doesn't matter since we'll be leaving soon, anyway."

"How long do you need to set up the protection spell?"

"It will take me at least a couple of days," she replied.

"Dante promised to contact me again today. He'll be in this area as early as tomorrow, so that timing will work out perfectly. When he's closer, we can decide where to meet him."

"We need to talk Alaric into helping us," she stated.

"That won't be easy," I argued.

Alaric might not be willing to claim Serena as his mate, but he also wasn't willing to let her go.

"We'll need someone to help us get away from here if the leadership council is determined to keep us from leaving," she pointed out.

"I suppose you're right," I agreed. "I'll try to come up with a way to deal with Alaric while you finish the spell."

"It might be best if we both talk to him," she suggested.

I started to open my mouth to argue, but Serena was right. A united front would be best. "Okay, we'll talk to him together."

Chapter Twenty-Five

"You want me to do what?"

Alaric had reacted exactly as I'd expected. The last time we'd spoken to him, we'd both told him off, and now we were asking for his help. We were asking him to break more rules and defy his council.

Serena rolled her eyes and put her hands on her hips as she responded to him. "You heard what Juliet asked."

"I know we're asking a lot of you," I told him. "I understand why you'd want to turn us down. Helping us would mean breaking a bunch of rules, not to mention you know this means losing Serena. I know you don't want her to leave."

Alaric put a hand up and shook his head. "No, this has nothing to do with my feelings for Serena, though I am worried about her safety."

"Are you refusing to help us?" she asked.

Alaric snorted and muttered something under his breath that I couldn't quite make out. "I should refuse to help you. All helping you has done is cause trouble for me. Do you know what they're starting to say about me here?"

"What are they saying?" I asked.

"There are several people who believe I may have been compromised by my time in captivity," he replied. "You aren't the only ones having their motives and loyalty challenged. I'm getting some leeway because of my mother, but that won't last long. Now, you want me to help you leave after the council refused to grant permission. You could leave us vulnerable to attack from an enemy we aren't sure how to fight. Do you think I'll betray my people for you? I'm not going to let more children die."

Serena's face softened for the first time since Alaric had entered the cabin. "I know how it feels to be treated like an outcast and to have your motives questioned by your people no matter what you do. I hate that helping us has caused you so many problems."

Alaric moved closer and reached out as if to touch her cheek, but she stepped out of his reach. His hand dropped to his side as he let out a sigh and looked at the ground.

"I don't regret helping you, Serena. It's more complicated than regret. With all that's going on, I'm not sure that I'll be able to protect you here, yet I can't let you leave us with no defenses."

"We're leaving no matter what anyone here says," Serena told him. "I've already started weaving a protection spell into your perimeter spells."

"You have?" he asked. "When did you have time for that?"

"All we have is time," I reminded him. "Serena has been working hard to keep the children safe. This will be better protection against those creatures. We can't follow the children around all day and night."

Alaric nodded. "Yes, a protection spell is a better solution. Thank you." He met Serena's gaze. "Am I part of the reason you want to leave?"

"You're an idiot," Serena said under her breath. "I don't want to talk about us, and don't correct me by telling me there was never any *us*. For now, I need to focus on helping Juliet. You have nothing to do with my reasons for leaving."

"I have to help my people," I reminded him. "It will be a lot easier if you agree to help us, but we aren't changing our minds even if you refuse. All I ask is that you don't tell anyone we're planning to leave no matter what you decide."

"I also need someone to help me walk the perimeter without being disturbed," Serena added. "It will make it easier to finish setting up the protection spell. It's a complex spell, and it's harder when I keep getting interrupted. Your leadership council should be okay with this request since it will help protect the children from the soul eaters."

"Soul eaters?" he asked.

"The creatures who attacked the children," I explained.

Alaric's eyes narrowed. "I thought you didn't know what they were?"

"We didn't," I replied. "The demon with Dante recognized them from the description shared with her. She was also able to give some advice on how to protect your land. I can channel a small amount of Dante's magic to help Serena set up the protection spell faster."

"Demon? The warlock has a demon with him?"

I nodded. "That surprised me as well."

"Are you going to help us?" Serena asked.

"I'll help you set up the protection spell," he began. "As for you leaving? It's a terrible idea—one that could get us all killed."

"Your people will kill you for helping us?" I asked.

He shook his head. "I meant we could get killed after we leave."

"You aren't going with us," Serena argued.

His expression turned fierce. "Do you think I have a choice?"

Serena opened her mouth to respond, but Alaric spoke first.

"I can't be with you because you're a spellcaster. That makes me sound like a jerk, but it's the truth. I know I'm hurting you, and I hate that. Even though I can't have you, I also cannot allow you to walk into danger without me. My wolf is clawing at the surface and demanding I protect you."

"Allow me?" Serena asked angrily.

"I didn't mean that the way it sounded," he insisted with a smile. "What I meant is that I'm not going to sit around here while you put yourself at risk. I'm going to find a way to help you."

Serena's lips parted ever so slightly as she regarded Alaric. She didn't seem to know what to say in response, and I didn't blame her.

Alaric cleared his throat and said, "Give me some time to see what I can do. I'll take you around to set up the spell later today, but getting you out of here will take longer."

"You have two days to come up with a solution," I told him. "We're leaving in four."

"I'll do my best," he assured me before turning and walking out of the cabin.

"I thought we were leaving the day after tomorrow at the latest," Serena remarked, her gaze still on the door. "Did you lie to Alaric because you don't trust him?"

"I don't doubt his sincerity, but I can't risk having him try to stop us."

"I hope he helps us," Serena stated. "It will make things a lot easier. If he betrays us, I may have to put a spell on him to make him cluck like a chicken for the rest of his life."

"Can you really do that?" I asked with a laugh.

"Not the rest of his life," she admitted. "But I could make the next week rather embarrassing for him."

Chapter Twenty-Six

It took us nearly two days to set up the perimeter spell, which put us off schedule. Dante was also running later than expected, having had to alter his route.

Alaric hadn't given us any clues regarding his decision to help us. In fact, he kept putting the discussion off, claiming to be too busy.

"He's not going to help us," Serena said with a sad sigh.

"It's beginning to look that way," I agreed.

"It's probably better if we go without him," she stated.

I nodded. "His help would make it easier, but I'm not sure it was fair to ask him."

"You're right," she replied. "As much as his rejection makes me mad, I do appreciate all he's done for us."

A knock at the door interrupted us, and when I went to answer it, I found Alaric on the other side.

"We were just talking about you," I told him as I gestured for him to enter.

"All good, I hope," he replied.

Serena snorted. "Do you want us to lie?"

He laughed, but it lacked genuine humor. "Yes, I do. I can't help you leave in two days."

"I'm not all that surprised," I told him. "I knew there

was only a slim chance you could help us."

"We don't blame you," Serena added.

Alaric flashed her a warm smile. "I would blame myself. I have six others who will be traveling with us when we leave today."

"Today?" I asked with a quirked eyebrow. "That's not when I told you we're leaving."

"And I knew you were lying," he replied. "It makes more sense for us to leave now before anyone on the council decides to step up their guard on you."

"If you help us, you may not be able to come back here," Serena warned him. "Have you considered all you're risking? Do the people you recruited to help us know what's at stake?"

He nodded. "They know, but it's the right thing to do."

Serena studied him, clearly doubting his words. "Are you and the others ready to leave now?"

Alaric looked surprised by her question. "Don't you want to wait until tonight? It will be easier to sneak away when it's dark."

I shook my head. "No, it will be easier to sneak away during the day. At night, it will look suspicious if we wander off into the wooded area. We've been going for walks every day, so it will look like part of our normal routine. You have too many guards around at night for us to go unnoticed."

"Good point," he agreed. "I hadn't given any thought to the guards at night."

"That's because you aren't used to having anyone question your movements at night," Serena pointed out.

"True," he agreed. "I have been known to go for a run in wolf form at night, and no one has ever stopped me. Though I'm not sure if that would be the case now with some questioning my motives."

"All the more reason for us to leave in broad daylight," I stated.

"I'll gather the others," Alaric told us.

"We'll head out as soon as they're ready," I replied. "I

think we should leave in groups, and you shouldn't be with us."

Alaric's gaze shifted to Serena, and I knew he wanted to argue. He didn't like being away from her, and he didn't trust anyone else to keep her safe.

"She's right," Serena agreed. "If you go with us, it will look more suspicious."

"Are you sure you want to do this?" I asked. "You don't know what will happen to you if you leave with us."

"I'll be welcomed back here no matter what I do," he insisted.

I wondered if he truly believed that.

"When you leave, make sure everyone in your group is fully-clothed," Serena told him.

"Why would we want to travel in this form?" he asked as he gestured to his human form. "We're much better fighters and can move faster in our animal forms."

"You're in more danger from hunters in animal form," I pointed out. "The reason Dante didn't recognize me as a shapeshifter at first was that I was fully clothed and in my human form. The spellcasters don't expect to see us moving around like this."

"You also may need clothing at some point," Serena added. "I can always carry clothing for you after we leave here, but it would look more than a little suspicious if I went for a walk carrying a large bag of clothes."

Alaric nodded with a thoughtful expression on his face. "I don't know why I never considered that shapeshifters are much less conspicuous in human form."

"I'd like to leave here within the next hour," I told Alaric.

He nodded. "I'll send someone to go with you soon." He paused with his hand on the doorknob and looked over his shoulder at Serena. "Be careful."

"You too," she replied. "I'll be even angrier with you if you get hurt or killed."

Alaric flashed her a smile and said, "I'll keep that in mind."

Chapter Twenty-Seven

I didn't care much for the two shapeshifters Alaric sent to accompany us. One was male and the other female. Neither introduced themselves or spoke more than a few words as we walked farther from the rebel shapeshifter settlement.

The male was a couple of inches under six-feet-tall with broad shoulders and tanned skin. His dark brown hair went to just past his ears and curled slightly at the ends. He had amber eyes and full lips that seemed almost constantly pressed together in a disapproving line.

The female was nearly as tall as him with blonde hair that barely touched her shoulders. Her skin was also tanned. She had high cheekbones and pale blue eyes. Her angry scowl reminded me of Nidia's. Hopefully, her disdain for me wouldn't result in her betraying me as well.

It's not that I cared so much about making friends with the shapeshifters, but I wasn't sure I could trust them to have our backs. If they hated us, they'd be more inclined to let us die despite any loyalty they felt toward Alaric.

"What was Alaric thinking?" I asked under my breath.

"We have to trust Alaric," Serena whispered as she looked at our reluctant guides. "He wouldn't have sent these shapeshifters to help us if he didn't think we could trust them."

"You do realize that as shapeshifters we have a much keener sense of hearing, don't you?" the female asked Serena.

"Yes," Serena replied with a sweet smile. "I know you can hear us, but I chose to whisper so you wouldn't think I was talking to you." She frowned. "That sounded a lot ruder than I intended. You clearly don't want to talk to us, so I figured there was no reason to make you think you have to be a part of our conversation."

The male glared at us. "We're trying to avoid saying too much until we get farther from the settlement. There shouldn't be any guards out this way, but I prefer to avoid taking any chances."

"Look on the bright side. I don't think they plan to kill us," I told Serena in a conversational tone.

"I don't believe they *could* kill us," Serena remarked.

I stopped walking when I felt Dante's magic moving along mine as if he was reaching out to me. He wasn't trying to communicate with me telepathically so much as locate me. I closed my eyes and focused on the threads.

"He's close," I whispered.

"Dante?" Serena asked.

I nodded, suddenly unable to speak as the magic pulled me toward it. Energy flowed around me, invading every cell of my body. It vibrated along my skin and was so intense I heard it like the buzzing of a thousand bees.

"What's wrong with her?" the male demanded.

It sounded as if he was far away, though I knew he stood close to me.

"I don't know," Serena admitted as she caught my arm.

Her touch grounded me, and I no longer felt as if I were drowning in Dante's and my combined magic.

"Are you okay?" Serena asked.

I nodded and swallowed hard before responding. "I'm better now, but it might be best if you keep your hand on me. Something crazy is going on with Dante's magic. I need to talk to him before we go any farther."

"We don't have time to make a detour," the male argued. "You can figure out how to meet up with your warlock after we get to the spot where we're meeting Alaric and the others."

"I don't need to go to Dante to speak to him," I told the male with an exasperated sigh. "Just give me a minute, and then we'll be on our way again."

I didn't wait for a response before reaching out to Dante with my mind. There was no point in arguing. I had to do something about the magical pull, or it would slow us down.

"You're close."

"Yes," he replied. *"I can feel you, and it's making me crazy. Can you follow our connection to reach me?"*

"I have to meet the others who are helping us first," I told him. *"Is there any way you can stop whatever you're doing?"*

"Can you be a little more specific?" he asked.

"It feels like you're doing something with our bond," I explained. "I'm having trouble walking or hearing much of what's going on around me. It's too intense. Serena's holding my arm to keep me grounded."

"I'm not entirely certain what's causing that, but I'll stop tracking you for a short time and see if that helps. I can't stand around here much longer. Can you tell me what direction you're heading?"

"We're traveling northeast toward Jasmine Springs. We're supposed to meet by a copse of elms. Does that help?"

"I'm pretty sure I know where that is. At least, I'll be able to head in the right direction," he replied. *"When I get closer, I may need to trace your magic again to find your exact location. Our bond gets more intense the closer I get to you."*

"I'm almost afraid to see what it will be like when we're together. It didn't feel like this the last time."

"Hopefully, the intensity will let up once we're together again," he replied.

"If not, we'll have to figure something out. I really need to go. The shapeshifters with us are glaring at me."

"All right," he agreed. *"I'm shutting down our bond for now."*

"Are you done making that constipated face?" the male asked.

"Constipated?" I looked at Serena. "Did I really look constipated while I was talking to Dante?"

"A little," she admitted. "Is Dante okay?"

"Yes. I think I'll be okay to walk without your hand on me now, but grab my arm if you see me acting strange again. Dante is shutting down our bond in the hopes it will ease the intensity."

"All right," she agreed as she released my arm. "Let's go."

"It's about time," the male grumbled as he stalked ahead of us.

"Is it just me, or is he moody?" Serena asked loud enough for the shapeshifters to hear us. "He seemed a lot nicer at first. I don't think either of them like us, but at least he wasn't this testy."

I bit back my smile. "What? I thought they loved us and wanted to be our new besties. Do you really think they don't like us?"

"I can see why you might not have noticed their feelings," she replied with a grin. "They hide their irritation well."

The male stopped and spun to glare at us. "You may think this is a game, but Alaric is one of my closest friends, and I don't want to lose him. When the Azureans captured him, we were all sure we'd never see him again. I appreciate that you helped save my friend, but I don't appreciate all the danger you brought to my home. I'm only doing this for Alaric, not to become your friend."

"Fair enough," Serena agreed, not sounding the least bit annoyed. "As long as you don't betray us, we'll be fine."

"And what if I betray you?" he asked.

"Then I'll make what we did to the soul eaters look like

a tickle fight," she replied.

I laughed. "You don't do in between, do you, Serena? You went from being afraid all the time to standing up to every threat."

"I like this much better," she replied.

Before I could respond, the grumpy male spoke. "I can't picture you being afraid of many things. I'm beginning to understand why Alaric is so fond of you."

That was an improvement. He didn't offer his name or say anything for the remainder of the afternoon, but he seemed less irritated.

Chapter Twenty-Eight

We met up with the other shapeshifters four hours later. Alaric didn't look happy, not that I'd expected him to with the risk to him and his friends.

"Did you have any problems getting here?" Alaric asked as he approached us.

"If you don't count the shapeshifter freaking out and then making us stop so she could have a mental chat with her warlock, then everything went fine," the grumpy male replied.

Alaric frowned. "She has a name, Geori."

We had a name to go along with the grumpy personality.

"I know," Geori replied. "What difference does it make what I call her?"

"Hopefully, the other shapeshifters with us are less hostile," Serena stated. "I wouldn't want to have more like the two of you with us if there's a fight."

"Same here," I agreed. "It's never smart to have people who hate you at your back."

Alaric let out a frustrated sigh before glaring at Geori. "You and Elena didn't have to come with us. I told you that if you can't keep your attitude in check, you should stay behind."

"I'm trying," Geori insisted. "It's hard to accept that we're putting ourselves at risk for such a stupid reason. Why should we help them? One is a spellcaster, and the other is basically a willing familiar. Don't get me wrong. I can see why you like the witch, but I still think it's a mistake to help her."

"Is this really the best you could do?" I asked Alaric. "I believe he'll have *your* back, but I don't trust him to help my people."

"Why do the Heathergate Refuge shapeshifters need help?" Geori demanded. "Are they having some sort of disagreement with the spellcasters? Can't they offer to donate more of their energy or perhaps help the spellcasters trap some of us?"

"You didn't tell him what's really going on?" Serena looked like she was about to smack Alaric.

He shrugged.

"That's not an answer," I told him.

"I thought it was a rhetorical question," he replied.

"It wasn't," Serena snapped. "Why didn't you tell him everything?"

"I was wondering the same thing," Geori added.

Alaric first responded to Geori. "You didn't ask me for details, so I didn't give you any." His attention shifted to Serena. "I didn't have a lot of time to explain everything." Finally, he looked at me. "Since we're all together, why don't you tell Geori your reason for needing to return to your old home. I think it will be a bonding experience for both of you. If I didn't think you could trust him at your back, I wouldn't have asked him to come with us."

He walked away, leaving me with Geori and Serena.

Geori spoke first. "He does this kind of stuff all the time. This isn't the first time I've heard the bonding experience line. Alaric doesn't believe I'll bond with anyone over one of these explanations, but he just loves to give people hope that we'll become friends."

"I take it you don't get along with others," I remarked. "Or is it because you really don't have much in common with those he expects you to bond with?”

“A little of both, but mostly the first,” he admitted. “So, what’s the deal with this ridiculous mission? I know your stepmother tried killing you, so why go back there? You don’t strike me as someone with a death wish.”

“My father might be in danger,” I began. “He may even be dead.”

Geori’s face softened. “I’m sorry. That can’t be easy for you. I lost my father years ago.”

“I’m sorry for your loss,” I replied softly.

He shrugged. “As I said, it was years ago. What do you hope to accomplish by returning to the Heathergate Refuge?”

“It would probably be best if I tell you the whole story,” I began.

“All right,” he agreed.

“My stepmother took my bracelet and dropped me in a familiar trap,” I began. “She wanted to get me out of the way so my younger brother, her son, can be the next leader. That’s how I ended up with my warlock.”

“That’s messed up,” he replied. “My stepdad isn’t great, but he’d never try killing me.”

“She didn’t exactly try killing me,” I pointed out.

“There are a lot of shapeshifters who would consider what she did much worse,” he stated. “I wouldn’t want to live as a slave to the Azureans.”

“Neither would I,” I admitted.

“She wanted Juliet to suffer,” Serena remarked angrily.

“Either that or she’s squeamish,” Geori suggested.

“Squeamish?” I asked.

“It would have been smarter to kill you,” he explained. “Even without your bracelet, she still runs the risk of someone at a trading post recognizing you or having heard of your disappearance.”

“I doubt she expected me to make it to a trading post,” I replied. “Even if I had managed to get there, that was my first time away from the Heathergate Refuge, so none of the spellcasters would have recognized me. I'm certain she did this to be cruel."

"She made a big mistake by putting you in a trap in human form," Geori remarked. "We don't travel in human form."

I nodded. "Even if she knew that, she couldn't have done anything about it unless I'd chosen to change to a cat. She may have planned to force me into cat form, but I ran."

"I'm assuming you want to return because you're the rightful ruler," Geori deduced. "She stole your birthright. You must also want revenge."

"It's not that," I argued. "To be honest, I never wanted to be the leader. The day my stepmother betrayed me, I'd argued with my father about that. It wasn't the first time. He's always told me it's my responsibility to lead my people, but I didn't get it before."

"I take it that's changed," he remarked.

"Yes, because the people at the Heathergate Refuge are my responsibility. My brother, Ellis, is young, but my father doesn't believe he has the temperament to lead. Maybe he will when he's older, but I don't think that will be the case with my stepmother's influence. I also don't know if she'll kill my father to put Ellis in charge earlier. It's just a big mess. I have to make sure my people are safe. Likely, I won't be able to stay, but I can help them get some stability by dealing with my stepmother and those who betrayed me."

Geori let out a tired sigh. "I understand why you feel you need to go back, and I might even respect you a little."

"Oh, joy," I said under my breath.

He let out a startled bark of laughter. "Is that sarcasm I detect?"

"Was that a genuine laugh?" Serena asked with raised eyebrows.

"Yes, don't get used to it," he told her. "I'm still not sure I like or trust either of you."

Something told me he was lying. His tone had already changed.

"As long as you don't betray us, I don't care if you like us," I stated. "Now, if you'll excuse me, I need to figure out where my warlock is."

Chapter Twenty-Nine

The closer Dante got to us, the more intense our bond felt, though it was nowhere near as overwhelming as it had been earlier that day. It had remained open since I'd contacted him, so it would be easier to find me.

Rather than feeling like an unbearable buzzing, it had settled into a warm hum. When we'd reopened the link, I'd felt overwhelmed initially, but Dante had helped ease my rising panic. The more I accepted the sensation, the more natural it felt.

It would help if I had someone to ask about what was happening, but no one I'd met had heard of a bond like ours.

Serena waved a hand in front of my face.

"Sorry," I told her. "Did you say something?"

"I was asking if you're okay," she replied. "You've been staring at the same section of trees for the last ten minutes."

I nodded, unable to look away from those trees. "Dante is close."

"That's good since Alaric is getting impatient to start moving. I'm glad Dante made it this far. I was worried."

"We won't have to wait much longer," I assured her. "Can you tell Alaric that Dante will be here soon? Can you also find out how long we'll need to travel? I'm sure Dante is even more exhausted than we are."

She laughed. "If I tell Alaric that Dante will be here soon one more time, his head might explode. I'm not in the mood to have him snap at me. We can ask him about how much farther we need to go after Dante gets here."

I glanced her way and smiled. "Sorry. I hadn't considered how he's been reacting to your updates."

"It's all right," she assured me. "I'm going to eat something before we have to head out again. Should I bring you something?"

I shook my head. "No, I'm not hungry."

"Okay." She headed back toward the shapeshifters.

It was another ten minutes before I saw Dante. His dark brown hair was messy, and there was some stubble on his chin. He looked dark, dangerous, and gorgeous.

I raced toward him and threw myself into his arms. He caught me and held me close.

Taking a deep breath, I let his scent wrap around me.

Our bond heated as it swirled around us. I could see it in vibrant shades of blue and green.

"I didn't think I'd ever see you again," he said in a ragged voice. "Being away from you has been the worst kind of torture."

"When I couldn't reach you for so long, I was terrified you were dead." I ran my fingers through his hair. "Serena told me it could be a dampening spell affecting our link, but as the days passed, I worried more."

He pulled away and looked down at me. "It was a very close call."

"Dante!" Serena raced toward us. "You're here! Even when Juliet said you were close, I worried you wouldn't find us before the shapeshifters insisted we move on."

"You look different," he remarked as he studied her.

"She's no longer clutching a knife," I pointed out.

"I miss it," Serena admitted. "It's not as easy fighting monsters without the knife. I have a new one in my sheath. It just doesn't feel as good in my hand."

"You did fine fighting monsters without a knife," I reminded her. "I think you're even more powerful when you rely on magic."

Dante nodded. "For some creatures, like the soul eaters, that's true. I hear you saved a lot of children, cousin."

Serena blushed. "It wasn't just me. Juliet helped. You also helped with your magic."

"Ignore her modesty," I told Dante. "She was the first to get to the clearing, and she charged right in. Her quick action saved the lives of several children."

"I couldn't save them all," she replied with a sad smile before her attention shifted to the large dog sitting by Dante's side. "Is this the demon Juliet told me about?"

"Yes, this is Sin," Dante replied as he reached down to stroke the demon's back. "Sin has been a great help to me. I'm not sure I would have made it this far without her."

I felt a mix of gratitude and jealousy toward the demon.

Of course, I was grateful to her for helping Dante, but I was jealous of the time she'd spent with him and of the obvious bond they shared.

I needed to shake off my jealousy. We had no time for it.

"What's wrong?" Dante asked as he studied me.

I shrugged. "Where should I start? Both shapeshifters and spellcasters want me dead."

"Not all of them," Serena argued. "Maybe half."

"I don't think that's helping," Dante told her. "This close to you, I can feel a lot of what you are, but I can't interpret all of those feelings."

"That's a good thing," I told him. "Can you imagine how annoying it would be to have someone always know what you're feeling?"

"Yes, but it would be more convenient," he argued. "Especially when I feel like there's more bothering you."

I wrapped my arms around his waist and leaned into him, allowing his touch to soothe me as he rubbed my back. "A lot is going on, and I'm not sure my feelings make sense. Let me enjoy having you here with me."

"Of course," he agreed as he rested his chin on top of my head. "You feel so good in my arms. I'm never letting you go again."

Out of the corner of my eye, I saw Alaric and Geori stalking toward us.

"We need to head out now," Alaric snapped. "I know this joyful reunion may make you think things are going well, but they aren't."

Serena rolled her eyes. "Must you continue acting like a warthog's backside?"

"A warthog's backside?" he sputtered out.

I heard a snort of laughter from Dante as Geori cleared his throat.

"Yes," Serena replied. "I'm tired of this nasty attitude you've had since we met up with you. We're grateful for your help, but you could have sent us on our way if this was going to be such a problem for you."

Alaric let out a frustrated growl. "You're impossible."

"And you're acting moodier than Geori," she accused. "That's no easy feat."

Geori grinned. "I told you I wasn't the only one who noticed your foul mood today, Alaric."

Alaric glared at Geori. "Why don't you do something useful?"

"Why don't you stop bossing everyone around?" Serena asked Alaric.

Alaric looked furious, and his jaw ticked as he glared at Serena.

Dante was looking between the two of them with narrowed eyes. "What is going on between the two of you?"

"Nothing," Serena replied with a sweet smile. "Alaric wouldn't stoop so low as to involve himself with a witch. He's too good for that, but he's probably right about us needing to get moving."

She turned on her heel and started walking toward the trail with Geori by her side.

"Why can't you stop triggering her?" I asked Alaric. "Serena needs to focus on her surroundings so she can watch for any danger. She doesn't have time to worry about the drama between the two of you. Just stay away from her."

Alaric let out a frustrated sigh as he ran his fingers through his messy brown hair. "It's a little hard to stay away from her when we're all traveling together, but don't worry. I'll leave her alone as soon as I get the two of you someplace safe."

He walked in the direction Serena and Geori had gone—stomped actually better described his gait.

Dante shook his head. "This can't be good. I can't believe he thinks he's too good for her."

"I wish it was that simple," I replied.

Dante looked at me and then back at the trail where Alaric had headed. "This is a story I need to hear. We should catch up with the others."

I caught his hand. "Sorry, we can't stay here longer. I was hoping you'd get at least a short break."

"It's all right," he assured me. "Alaric is right about us not staying here. I can walk a little farther."

"Maybe your demon can change into a horse and carry you," I said as I looked down at her.

Based on her growl, she didn't appreciate my suggestion.

Chapter Thirty

We walked for a little over two hours before Alaric glanced back at Dante and frowned. He stopped and checked out our surroundings.

"We should make camp for the night," he announced.

"But it's safer to travel at night," Geori argued. "We should try to make it past the Azurean hunting grounds before we stop."

"The warlock is too tired to go any farther," Alaric stated. "He's probably been on his feet all day."

"For much of the last seventeen hours," Dante admitted.

I frowned. "Then, we should have stopped earlier."

Dante shook his head. "Unless they changed the hunting rotation, the area we were passing through will have hunters out checking traps in the morning. We needed to keep moving as long as possible."

"Do you think they changed the hunting schedule after you left?" I asked. "It's possible Nicolas or your father were worried you'd tell someone about the rotation."

"That's not likely," Serena argued. "They changed it once when I was fourteen, and it threw off too many people in the family."

"I seriously doubt they'll make any changes," Dante

agreed.

"That's careless," Geori remarked.

"Not really," Serena argued. "I don't know any hunters other than Dante who remember the entire schedule. I doubt anyone realized he had it memorized. Since it's posted, no one needs to remember the whole thing. Hunters usually only remember the areas they're responsible for. I'm honestly shocked you remember it, Dante. It's not the same each week."

"But it always follows the same pattern," he explained.

"Is this a good spot?" Alaric asked him.

Dante nodded. "There aren't any traps near here. It's not an area we usually hunt. It got removed from the rotation because it was always a waste of time."

Alaric nodded. "Yes, we don't often come this way. We'll set up camp. I can't have you getting too tired and not warning us about any traps. Your mind needs to be sharp."

"Ah, so a spellcaster can be useful," Serena said under her breath.

Alaric glared at her briefly but said nothing before barking out orders to the others.

"It's a little cold," Elena remarked. "Do you think we can get away with building a fire?"

"Too risky," Alaric told her.

"Only if you use real fire," Dante stated.

"You want to use a make-believe fire?" Geori asked with a sneer. "Then, we can all pretend to be warm."

"Don't be a jerk," Serena told him. "He's talking about creating a magical flame."

"Exactly," Dante agreed. "It will produce more heat than a regular fire, and no one will be able to see it from a distance."

The other shapeshifters look fascinated.

"No one can see it?" Geori sounded skeptical.

"No one more than about thirty feet away," Dante replied.

"This I have to see," Elena remarked.

"While you do that, I'm going to set a perimeter alarm

spell so no one sneaks up on us."

All but Dante spun to face Sin, who was suddenly in human form and fully clothed. She wasn't that much taller than me and had pale skin, deep red hair, and even deeper red eyes. She laughed at our shocked expressions before saying, "Demon magic is always better."

After she skipped off to set up the spell, I asked, "How did she have time to dress? She was still a dog when I looked over a minute ago."

"Where was she carrying the clothing?" Alaric asked. "She didn't touch your pack, and she wasn't carrying anything."

"She can just appear fully clothed," Dante explained. "Sometimes, her human appearance changes. The only constant seems to be her red eyes. I asked her to stick to one human form. In animal form, she has more control over her eye color."

"What's her true form like?" Geori asked.

Dante shrugged. "Sin isn't big on sharing details about demons. She tells me what she wants me to know and turns into a dog if I ask about something she doesn't want to discuss. That's her preferred form."

"Is her name really Sin?" Geori asked.

"No, demons don't reveal their actual name," Dante replied as he crouched down and dropped his pack on the ground. His eyes closed as his hands hovered several inches above the ground.

As he softly spoke the words to the spell, I felt the tug of his magic, pulling on our bond to feed into his power. Panic gripped me until he spoke in my mind.

"Don't be frightened, Juliet. I'm not taking your power, just drawing on the energy we share."

I relaxed and nodded, watching as blue flames rose from the ground. The heat from the fire flowed around the area, taking away the slight chill that I hadn't noticed until we'd stopped walking.

"That should do it," Dante stated as he stood and rubbed his hands together.

"I don't see how we can hide this fire," Geori remarked. "I know it's supposed to have some special kind of magic, but this is too bright."

"As I said, it's only visible within a thirty-foot radius," he assured Geori. "If anyone gets close enough to see the fire, they can already see us."

"If Dante says you can't see it from more than thirty feet away, then I believe him," I stated. "You're welcome to check."

Geori nodded and started walking with three other shapeshifters. I could tell when they reached the spot where the flames vanished by their gasps.

"That's amazing," Geori said as he approached the flames again. "Not only could I no longer see it, but the heat disappeared."

Dante nodded. "I learned this spell as a young child. My father taught it to me when he took me camping. It's very useful."

"Can we cook on it if we catch any food?" Alaric asked.

"I wouldn't recommend it," Dante replied. "I tried it once, and the magic leaves a strange aftertaste."

"Dried meat it is," Alaric stated. "Let's all eat and try to get some sleep. We need to start moving in six hours tops."

The others started pulling food from their packs.

"Are you hungry?" I asked Dante.

He shook his head. "The nuts and jerky we ate while walking were enough for me. I need to get some sleep, yet I'm almost afraid to close my eyes. I don't want to wake up and find out this is all a dream, and I'm not really with you."

He pulled me into his arms and sighed as I rested my head against his chest.

"I know just how you feel," I admitted. "At least I get to finally sleep beside you again."

"Yes, I've missed having you with me," he replied before releasing me and looking down at the ground. "I'm getting tired of sleeping on the ground."

"Don't you have some sort of spell to make it more

comfortable?”

"No, I don't know any spells for that," he replied. "You're lucky you can sleep in your cat form. That should be more comfortable."

He was right; I would be more comfortable, but I didn't want to change into a cat.

"I want to hold you," I told him.

He smiled and brushed my hair back from my face. "Then let's see if we can make a comfortable bed with the blanket in my pack. We should be warm enough to use it as a pillow."

While he got our sleeping area set up, I went to check on Serena.

"You don't have to sleep so far from us," I told her.

She was sitting several feet away and had a small black dog that had to be Sin on her lap.

"It's okay," she assured me. "I want to give you and Dante some time alone. Sin growls every time Alaric comes near me."

I looked at the demon. "Not a fan of Alaric?"

All she did was lift one ear in response.

"Who would have thought a demon could offer so much comfort?" Serena asked with a giggle.

"That is somewhat unexpected," I agreed. "I'll see you in the morning."

When I returned to Dante, he was already lying on his back, watching my approach. He opened his arms and gestured for me to join him.

After I was settled in beside him with my head resting on his chest, I let out a sigh. "I'm glad your demon friend seems to like Serena."

"I think she may like Serena more than she likes me," he remarked.

"Doubtful," I replied. "I'm a little jealous of the bond you have with Sin."

"You have nothing to be jealous of," he assured me. "I'm in love with you, and there is no other woman for me."

"Why can't love be simple?" I asked.

"Life is rarely simple," he replied.

"Your life was a lot simpler without love. It's been torn apart since the day you decided to spare my life. Before that, you were a well-respected member of the spellcaster community. You were happy. Now, you can't go back to your family or your old life."

"My happiness depended upon my ignorance," he replied. "Sure, it was easier not knowing that hunting shapeshifters was wrong, but I'm glad my eyes were opened. I don't know what the future holds, but I don't want to return to my old life."

"What about Ambrose and Laranissa?" I asked. "Surely, there are others you miss."

"Yes," he whispered. "I miss them, but this is how it has to be. Get some sleep. Tomorrow will be another long day."

"Goodnight, Dante."

"Sweet dreams, Juliet."

Chapter Thirty-One

We covered more ground than expected the next day, thanks to Sin's suggestion of an alternate route.

Alaric had been more than a little suspicious of her directions—not that I blamed him. According to Sin, she'd never traveled to this area, yet she knew the location of the isolated spellcaster community. She also knew of a trail on none of our maps.

After much discussion, we'd opted to try the path she suggested since Dante was concerned we'd run into Azureans if we followed our planned route.

The trail would cut a few hours off of our trip, and though poorly maintained, it was still walkable. Everything was going well.

I should have felt relieved that we were closer to getting my new bracelet. Instead, I was tenser and more uneasy.

"Stop worrying so much," Serena told me from my right side.

Dante snorted. "Considering all we've dealt with, I think it's smart to worry. We don't know any of these spellcasters. They may not be willing to help us. Worse, they may turn us over to the Azureans."

"The one who can help you is a demon," Sin

announced as she skipped past us with her hands waving in the air.

"A demon?" I asked. "No one mentioned anything about a demon."

"The original magic for your bracelets was demon magic. It's been altered some by spellcasters," Sin called out from ahead of us.

"I'm not sure I like the idea of dealing with a demon," Alaric remarked.

Sin stopped and glared at him. "Why not?"

"Are you saying I should trust all demons?" Alaric asked.

Sin laughed. "Oh, no. You shouldn't trust any demon."

"Even you?" I asked.

"Even me," she replied before skipping ahead again.

"Isn't this demon worried about demon hunters?" Dante asked. "Or does this community have protection spells like the ones woven into the Black Mist?"

"Demons who live away from the protected areas aren't like me," Sin remarked as she slowed her pace and caught Dante's hand. "With demon hunters after them, they need to either hide or become scary enough to be left alone. This demon is good at going unnoticed, or so I've heard. It must be at least somewhat true. She'd already be dead if she was still as reckless as the last time I saw her."

"You know the demon we're meeting?" Dante asked.

"I wouldn't say I *know* her," Sin replied.

"Sin," Dante began in an impatient tone. "I know you like playing games, but we need any information you have so we can avoid getting ourselves killed."

"Fine," she relented. "This demon poses as a witch and sells spells to stay alive."

"Can you tell us anything else about her?" I asked.

"She hates demons," Sin replied thoughtfully. "I think she hates everyone. Children always irritated her. She loathed being in animal form."

"She sounds awful," Serena remarked.

"Yes, I suppose she is, but I don't think she'll be a big

threat to you," Sin assured her. "There is one thing to watch out for."

"What's that?" Dante asked.

"She's always been fascinated with death magic," Sin explained.

"Death magic?" Serena gasped. "That's horrible."

Sin waved off her concerns. "There's nothing wrong with a little death magic now and then. It can make a demon stronger, but people will find out and want us dead if we use it too often. We all worried she'd ruin our truce, and we'd be banished from our sanctuary, especially since she has a way of tricking people into agreeing to be her sacrifice." She looked at Dante over her shoulder. "Don't agree to help her with any spells."

"All right," Dante agreed. "So, she was banished for her use of death magic?"

"No," she replied. "Several of us thought she should be banished, but it never came to that. She chose to leave. I may have had something to do with her decision."

"How so?" Dante asked.

"It's a long story, and I'm already bored," Sin complained.

"Can you give us a few details?" Dante coaxed.

"I told her I'd destroy her if she broke the rules by using death magic again," she explained. "She got defensive."

"So, your presence may not be good for us," I stated.

"Why?" Sin asked with a bewildered expression.

"She might consider you an enemy," Serena pointed out. "You did threaten to destroy her."

Sin considered what she'd said before waving off Serena's words. "You're thinking like a spellcaster."

"She is a spellcaster," I reminded Sin.

"I suppose that makes it harder to see it from a demon's perspective," Sin remarked thoughtfully. "Demons don't feel the same loyalty to others. We don't get offended when someone betrays us, though we might kill them. We value our own survival above all others."

"Wouldn't that have prompted you to stay behind where you had more protection against demon hunters?" I asked.

She shook her head. "I've been so bored lately that I needed an adventure. This has been fun so far. Did you think I came because I like Dante?"

"Yes," I replied.

"I suppose I *do* like Dante, so much so that I hope I won't have to betray him, but it could happen," she explained. "I won't risk my life for anyone else."

"From what I've heard of the spellcasters in this community, they wouldn't tolerate death magic," Dante remarked. "Maybe you're mistaken and this demon is no longer there."

"More likely, the foolish spellcasters don't know about the death magic," Sin argued.

"They may not know about her being a demon," I suggested.

Sin shrugged. "Perhaps she'll tell us."

"Is there anything else we should know?" Dante asked. "I expected to be negotiating with spellcasters. I'm not sure how to negotiate with a demon."

Sin pondered his question before responding. "Don't agree to do her any favors in exchange for the bracelet. Make sure the payment is clearly discussed in advance. You also shouldn't take it personally if she threatens to kill you. We do that sort of thing even with people we like."

"Great," I grumbled. "This should be an interesting meeting."

"It's going to be fine," Dante assured me.

I looked over at him. "Do you believe that, or are you trying to make me feel better about this?"

"Do you really want me to answer?" he asked.

I sighed and shook my head. "No, I already know the answer."

Chapter Thirty-Two

Her name was Peony.

At least, that's what she went by. The name seemed wrong for a powerful demon who liked to dabble in death magic, but that might have been the reason she'd chosen it. Both her name and appearance made her seem less threatening.

Peony stood in front of a row of rustic cabins near a large fire pit. She was barely five-feet-tall with blonde hair that went past her waist. Thick lashes framed her pale blue eyes, and her pink lips were curled into a welcoming smile. She wore a light blue dress that flowed down around her petite frame and fell to just above her ankles.

Peony's blue eyes looked more human than Sin's deep red eyes, making me wonder if she'd found some spell to hide her eye color or if some demons simply had eyes that didn't stand out as much.

"Welcome to my haven." Her voice was soft with a hint of an accent I didn't recognize. "What can I do for you?"

"We need your help finding a particular item," Alaric explained.

Peony glared at him, and I could have sworn I saw a flash of red in her eyes, though I might have imagined it.

"You are not the one looking for help," she accused. "I

think the female can speak for herself."

Alaric seemed taken aback by her tone, but he simply nodded.

"I need to return to the Heathergate Refuge with my friends," I began.

She studied us before gesturing wildly to the others with me, "Are they really your friends?"

I shrugged. "Some are my friends, while others are not."

"And you want the ones who aren't friends to travel with you past the Ivorfalls, as well?" She didn't give me a chance to respond. "Are you planning to kill the shapeshifters there? If that's the case, then you should leave now. I don't need to bring that kind of trouble on myself. Besides, I have no good reason to kill the shapeshifters at the Heathergate Refuge. They bring me peaches and plums in the summer months."

"You have dealings with the shapeshifters from the Heathergate Refuge?" I'd never heard of any trading done outside of the Azurean trading posts.

"It would probably be best if I ask the questions," she stated. "I'm not about to risk my own safety by helping you attack those shapeshifters."

"I don't want to attack them," I insisted. "Not all of them, anyway. I'm the daughter of the leader. My stepmother took my bracelet and left me in an Azurean trap so her son could be the next leader. I'm worried my father and those loyal to him will die if my stepmother isn't stopped."

Peony didn't speak, and I wasn't sure if she was waiting for me to say more.

"You should help her," Sin announced.

I hadn't realized she'd followed us until she spoke. We'd all agreed that it would be best if Sin stayed outside the settlement. Even she'd agreed that she should stay behind, and yet there she stood, possibly angering the demon who could help me get past the Ivorfalls.

Peony's blue eyes narrowed as her gaze landed on Sin.

"What are you doing here? More importantly, what did you tell them?"

Sin laughed off her anger. "Relax, Peony. I gave them a brief history but nothing they can use against you. Of course, I would never tell them your actual name. I know you're going to want to help them, so I wouldn't even consider threatening to reveal something so personal."

That certainly sounded like a threat.

"Why are you with them?" Peony demanded. "You never cared enough to get involved with anyone else's problems. You lorded your power over us and hid in your puppy form."

"A lot has changed," Sin replied with a sigh. "My life has been drudgery for centuries, but this warlock fascinates me." She gestured to Dante. "It seemed like a delightful adventure, so here I am."

Peony's full attention shifted to Dante. "Who are you?"

"Dante Verdugo," a warlock called out from behind us.

We all turned toward the warlock who'd spoken, and I gasped.

"Juliet Shadow Walker, it's good to see you again."

"Erik," I began cautiously. "What are you doing here?"

"Same as you," he replied. "Various things I don't want either the Azureans or Tulureans to know about."

"Ah, so you know each other," Peony said with a bright smile. "Erik is another fascinating warlock."

"It seems he is," Dante said under his breath.

Erik grinned. "I'm glad you're okay. We were worried when we heard about what happened with Juliet. That took me by surprise. Juni tried pretending she wasn't, but I could tell she was just as shocked."

"So, you know I'm not Juliet Shadow Walker."

"I know you're a shapeshifter," Erik confirmed. "That didn't come as nearly as much of a shock as Dante's part in helping you."

"Enough chatter," Peony snapped. "I've been asked to get Juliet and her shapeshifter companions past the Ivorfalls."

"I need to pass with the spellcasters and Sin," I added.

Peony let out a humorless laugh. "Oh, no. I already told you I'm not going to help you attack those shapeshifters. I can't see any other reason for bringing the spellcasters with you."

"I'm not trying to hurt my people, and neither are they," I insisted.

"I don't know," she hedged.

Erik frowned. "Why do you want to go to the Heathergate Refuge?"

"Some silly nonsense," Peony replied with a dismissive wave of her hand. "I think she feels loyal to her people. I don't know what would possess her to think that bringing hunters there would be a good idea."

"They're no longer hunters," I argued. "Serena was never a hunter."

"That's true," Erik agreed. "Both Dante and Serena have been sentenced to death for helping Juliet."

Peony looked perplexed. "But the Verdugos are merciless killers."

"Are you claiming you aren't a killer?" Sin asked.

Peony snorted. "You don't know me anymore. What name do you go by now?"

"Sin."

"That's appropriate," Peony said with a laugh before gesturing around her. "These are my people. They are my family, my children."

"Do they know the truth?" Sin asked.

"We know," Erik replied.

"What is your relationship to all of this, Erik?" Dante asked. "You live in Azuredale, and you've worked at the disposal center since before your voice changed."

"It's easier to slip away from there," Erik replied. "I'd rather not go into details. If you get caught, I don't want you letting anything slip that might get people I care about killed."

"I understand," Dante replied.

"Will you help me?" I asked. "I know I'm asking a lot,

and you have no reason to trust me, but I promise I'm really trying to do what's best for my people at the Heathergate Refuge."

"And what will you give me in exchange for my help?" Peony asked as she regarded me with a calculating gleam in her eyes. Her attention then shifted to Dante. "Or you? Do you truly want to help this shapeshifter? Am I supposed to believe you don't consider her a familiar for you to drain?"

Dante met her gaze. "I love Juliet, and I'd be willing to die for her."

"No!" Sin shouted. "Did you not listen to anything I said on the way over here? Telling her you would die to keep Juliet safe is the same as making an offer."

Peony laughed. "I promise I won't consider that an offer. In my new life, I've learned to negotiate like a witch. I didn't ask this to trick him, though I can see why you might suspect I would. This situation fascinates me. I've seen a spellcaster fall in love with a shapeshifter before, but it doesn't happen often. I suppose it makes more sense in this case."

"Why is this situation different?" I asked.

"Get them something to eat and find them all places to sleep tonight, Erik," she commanded as she stood and hurried into one of the cabins without answering my question.

"Do you know why she thinks my situation is different?" I asked Erik.

He shrugged. "I don't have a clue, but you likely won't get an answer. She does that a lot."

Sin laughed. "She's mellowed."

I let out a tired sigh. "Do you think she'll help us?"

"Of course," Sin replied. "She's delaying so she can watch you longer. You really are fascinating creatures."

"Yes, fascinating," Erik said softly with the same shy smile he'd had when he'd first tried flirting with me. He cleared his throat and looked away. "We'd better get you fed and settled in for the night. I need to get back to

Azuredale before my absence is noticed."

"You aren't going to tell them we're here, are you?" Dante didn't sound all that worried.

Erik shook his head. "That wouldn't end well for any of us."

"No, it certainly wouldn't," Dante agreed.

Chapter Thirty-Three

Though I enjoyed having a comfortable bed for the night, I couldn't get my mind to shut off. Dante and Serena had fallen asleep hours ago.

I wasn't sure where Sin had gone or if she planned to share the cabin with us at some point. She'd disappeared shortly after our meeting with Peony.

Rather than pacing the small cabin and risking waking Dante or Serena, I slipped outside to go for a walk. After strolling a short distance, I took a seat on a log facing a large pond where the full moon was reflected on the water.

I was there for around ten minutes before I heard footsteps approaching.

"You should be sleeping," Geori remarked from behind me.

I quirked an eyebrow as he sat beside me on the log. "Were you ordered to check on me?"

"There's no one awake to order me. It's my turn to stand guard, and I decided to see why you're brooding instead of sleeping."

"Brooding?" I asked. "I'm not brooding."

"Then what are you doing?" he asked as he regarded me.

I shrugged. "I can't sleep."

"Because you don't trust the demon?" he asked.

"Sin isn't at the cabin," I replied. "I'm not sure where she is."

"I meant the other demon."

I shrugged. "She hasn't done anything to make me distrust her."

"She hasn't done anything to earn your trust either."

"I'm at a point where I can't always wait for people to earn my trust, but you are right about me not being certain I can trust her. It doesn't help that Sin told us we can't trust demons."

"After all you've been through, it's probably hard trusting anyone."

"Since when are you an expert on me?" I asked.

"I don't need to be an expert to know this about you," he stated. "People you probably knew your entire life betrayed you, so why would you have any faith in those you just met? How were you able to trust Dante and Serena?"

"Why do you want to know?"

He shrugged. "I just want to understand you better."

"Because you want to better understand your enemy?"

Enemy might be too strong of a word, but Geori didn't seem fond of me.

He chuckled. "I don't think of you as my enemy. You created many problems for my community, and I don't like that, but I'm starting to like you. You aren't a coward, and Serena feels you deserve her loyalty. Serena has a lot of reasons to distrust others, too, especially our kind. Do you think she could ever truly trust another shapeshifter after what happened?"

"She trusts me."

He shifted uncomfortably. "Yes, she does. I meant a different kind of trust, more like what you share with your warlock."

"Ah! Now, I understand what this is about. You like Serena, and you want to get on my good side so I'll tell you more about her."

I respected him more when he didn't deny my

accusation.

"I shouldn't like her. My family would never approve, and she's so unlike me. Alaric also has feelings for her, though he may never act on them. It's a mistake to want anything with her. I should stay away from her."

"Right," I began in a clipped tone. "You sound like Alaric. It's going to be hard, so why even try to make it work? That's what you're saying, isn't it? You should both leave Serena alone because she's a spellcaster and too much trouble."

Geori put his hands up in surrender. "Whoa! I think you're reading a lot more into what I said than you should."

"You just said you can't like her because your family would disapprove," I argued.

He shook his head. "No, I said, I *shouldn't* like her. You're assuming that because my family wouldn't approve that I would turn my back on Serena. I can see why you feel that way, considering how Alaric is behaving. I don't get close to others, but I want to get to know her better. I feel like I should keep that to myself because I know she has feelings for Alaric, and she's under enough stress already. I don't want to add to that."

Wow!

I would not have guessed Geori could be so sensitive.

"Sorry, I overreacted," I replied. "Serena is amazing. Any male would be lucky to have her in his life."

"I think she loves Alaric," he said with a sad smile.

"No, she doesn't love him, but she is drawn to him," I replied with a frustrated sigh. "I know he's one of your closest friends, but he's such a jerk. It would help if he'd stop acting jealous and possessive around her."

"He's not acting," Geori replied with a bark of laughter. "Alaric is jealous of any time I spend around her, even if he's the one who told me to guard her. He feels very possessive when it comes to Serena."

"That's messed up. He's the one who pushed her away."

"I don't want to talk about Alaric," he told me. "He's

like a brother to me, and I owe him a lot. Even if I think he's wrong where Serena is concerned, I'm not going to sit here and bad mouth him."

"But you're considering pursuing a relationship with Serena?"

"Someday, I'd like to," he admitted. "Now isn't the right time. The last thing I want is for Serena to have more stress. Alaric would also be a lot more distracted if I started showing any obvious interest in her."

"I respect you more for thinking of these things," I stated. "Don't hurt Serena, or I'll make you wish you'd never been born."

"I'll do my best," he replied. "Do you think I might have a chance with her? I've seen how she looks at Alaric."

"I don't know," I admitted. "Was checking on me a ruse to ask about Serena?"

He shook his head. "No, I really did want to check on you. Tomorrow is going to be a long day, and you need to get some sleep."

"But not you?" I asked.

"I only have a two-hour watch," he replied.

"I can take over the rest of your watch," I offered.

"Alaric would be angry if I let that happen," he replied.

"Right, why trust me?"

"It's not a matter of trusting or not trusting you. Alaric gets angry when any of us defy his orders."

I let out a sigh as I stared out at the water again. "Then I guess I'll try getting to sleep again."

"Goodnight, Juliet," he said as he stood and walked away.

I stood and stretched before heading back to the cabin.

Once inside, I laid beside Dante, and he murmured something sleepily as he pulled me close. I didn't immediately drift off to sleep, but eventually, my eyes closed, and my breathing steadied.

Sadly, my sleep was not nearly as restful as I'd have liked.

Chapter Thirty-Four

Despite my horrible night's sleep, I felt well-rested when I awoke the next morning. I suspected it had a lot to do with having a comfortable bed and Dante by my side.

"Good morning," Dante murmured from my side.

"Good morning. I love waking up with you by my side."

"Me too," he agreed. "Where is Serena?"

"I heard her leave about twenty minutes ago," I replied. "Since I'd just woken up, I didn't get a chance to ask her where she was going, but she probably went to get something to eat."

"Then I have you all to myself for a little while," he replied. "This is nice."

"It is nice. I was so terrified I'd never see you again, terrified you were dead. Sorry, I know I keep saying the same thing."

"It's okay," he assured me as he brushed my hair back from my face. "This is still bothering you."

"What happened? Obviously, you didn't get a slap on the wrist like you expected, or you wouldn't be on the run."

"Nicolas convinced the right people that I was plotting against the Azureans with rebel shapeshifters. That was enough to earn me a death sentence."

"Nicolas is such a lying toad," I grumbled.

"He had a lot to work with. I lied about who you were, and I helped Serena escape. I also used magic against my brother and helped Alaric escape. I was captured in the company of a rebel shapeshifter. In hindsight, I should have expected a harsh punishment."

"I'm sorry you lost so much helping me, Dante."

"Stop saying that. Before you opened my eyes to what was going on around me, I was nothing more than an executioner and a slave trader. That's the life I lost. Yes, things are a mess for us right now, but they won't be forever. We'll find a place where we can be together—a place where we're safe."

"Safe," I whispered. "Do you suppose we'll ever truly feel that way again? It's so hard trying to imagine a place where we can both be accepted."

"I wish I could give you reassurances."

"I don't need reassurances," I insisted. "Let's start with finding a place where we're safe and worry about being accepted later."

"Good idea," he agreed. "We should probably push Peony for some answers so we can get moving."

"You're right. I hate that we had to wait another day, even though it was probably a good idea to get some rest."

"You're such an impatient cat."

"That's one of my best qualities."

He quirked an eyebrow. "You're bragging about your impatience?"

"Of course," I told him as I stood and stretched. "I get things done because I hate waiting for them to happen."

"Good point," he agreed. "Let's track down Peony."

"Where do you suppose Sin is?" I asked as I looked around. "I was surprised when she didn't try sleeping in here last night. I mentioned she wasn't with us when I saw Geori, but I don't think he's seen her either."

"Geori?" he asked. "Did he stop by here?"

I shook my head. "I couldn't sleep, so I went for a walk."

"I'm surprised that didn't wake me up," he mused as he changed his shirt.

"Do you think Sin left?"

He shook his head. "I don't think she'd leave without me."

"She really likes you."

"It seems that way," he agreed. "Sometimes, she admits to it while to others she insists I'm just a curiosity."

"Has she ever tried kissing you?"

I tried keeping my voice light, as if it didn't matter to me one way or another, but I hated the idea of Sin trying to kiss Dante.

He slipped his arms around me and pulled me close until his lips brushed against mine in a feather-light kiss.

His arms remained around me as he looked down into my eyes. "You're the only one I'm interested in kissing. You know that, right?"

"I believe you," I assured him.

"Sin asked me to kiss her," he began. "I want to tell you she understood my reasons for turning her down, but demons don't see the world as we do. She didn't understand my desire to commit to just you, but she has respected my choice."

"I'm glad," I said as I stood on tiptoes and grabbed his hair so I could pull him closer.

His lips lingered on mine, and I savored his kiss for that short time.

When he broke the kiss, he kept his mouth close to mine as he asked, "Did Geori try kissing you?"

I laughed and swatted his chest. "No, he's another male shapeshifter who's fallen for your cousin."

"He has?" Dante's eyebrows shot up as he released me.

I nodded.

He considered what I'd said. "I like him better than Alaric."

I let out a bark of laughter. "Geori?"

"Yes, he may be moody, but he's not hurting my cousin."

"He's not as bad as I thought he was," I admitted.

"So, he plans to pursue Serena?"

"He's holding off on that," I began. "I think he's right to wait. Now's not the time."

"No, it's not," he agreed. "Let's go track down Peony."

Chapter Thirty-Five

It wasn't easy finding Peony.

"Peony!" I shouted when I saw the demon hurrying toward the wooded area behind her home.

She didn't stop or even acknowledge me.

"Gee," Dante began in a dry tone. "I'm starting to get the feeling she doesn't want to talk to us."

"You caught that too?" I asked as we raced after her.

"Why are you following me?" she demanded without sparing us a glance.

"Why are you trying to avoid us?" I asked.

She stopped walking and glared at me. "Why would I avoid you? Did it ever occur to you that I have other matters to attend to?"

"Peony," Dante began in a patient tone. "I understand you're busy, and I know helping us could put you in a difficult position."

"Yes, it could," she snapped. "I've worked hard to build my life here, and you want me to risk losing it all to help you. I don't even know you."

I glared at Dante, certain the demon was going to turn down our request after he'd mentioned her fears. He caught my hand and gave it a reassuring squeeze before continuing.

"I know you're probably worried we'll reveal the truth about your identity to those who may want to use it against you. You don't want the rest of the world realizing you're not a witch."

Her eyes narrowed. "Are you threatening to reveal my identity if I don't help you?"

Dante shook his head. "We have no interest in getting more innocent people killed. You aren't causing us or anyone in this area problems."

She let out a startled bark of laughter, still looking tense. "Innocent? I've never been accused of innocence."

"You aren't hurting anyone with your deception," I added.

Peony relaxed some and nodded. "I don't hurt many people, only those who deserve to be hurt. You shouldn't have come to me. It's not fair." She stomped her foot.

"I'm sorry my situation is causing you stress," I said honestly. "Until recently, I never appreciated how hard it could be to try to build a new life like you've done for yourself here. The day my stepmother betrayed me, I lost everything—my safety and my home. There isn't a safe place for me, so I understand your desire to feel secure. I'm sure Dante does as well. He can never return to his home."

She studied me before nodding. "Yes, you've both been through a lot. Do you honestly believe it will be safe for you in the Heathergate Refuge, even if you kill your stepmother? Do you think they'll accept you now that you're bound to a spellcaster? And what if they do? Can you step back into your old life? I couldn't, even if I was welcome. Sometimes, we change too much to ever go back."

"No, I can't just return to my old life. I'm no longer the same person," I admitted. "The changes aren't bad. I'll be able to make a real difference as the leader with my new knowledge."

"What about your warlock?" she asked. "Where is he supposed to be while you're making those changes? He's not a shapeshifter, and your people won't accept him."

"I didn't think I could accept a shapeshifter before I met Juliet," Dante stated. "I doubt Juliet believed she'd ever bring a spellcaster past the Ivorfalls. We can all change."

"Change." She spat out the word as if it left a foul taste in her mouth. "Few want change if it means giving up the hate that fuels them."

"You're right, but I'm not giving up Juliet, so they'll just have to get used to me being around. Are you going to help us?" Dante asked.

She hesitated before nodding. "I think you're fools for trying, but when you get yourselves killed, I'll no longer have to worry about you revealing my secrets. Now, if you'll excuse me, I have work to do. I'll make your bracelets later today, and you can set out on your suicide mission. How many do you need?"

"Nine," I replied.

I'd planned to travel with Dante, Serena, and Sin, but Alaric insisted that he and the other shapeshifters go with us.

She snorted. "Nine. She wants nine bracelets."

She spun on her heel and stalked away, but not in the direction she'd originally been heading.

She stopped and cursed before turning to wave an angry finger at us. "You're both a distraction!"

She stomped off in the right direction, still complaining under her breath.

"I think your speech touched her," Dante remarked.

I couldn't tell if he was joking or not, but I laughed at the suggestion of Peony being touched by anything. "No, I think she's hoping we'll get killed."

"Either way, we're getting what you want," he said.

I frowned. "This isn't what you want, is it?"

He shrugged. "I want to be with you, and I know this is important to you."

"If you could go anywhere with me, where would you go?"

"I'd take you and Serena back to the place where I met

Sin," he replied without hesitation. "That's not an option. Neither of us can hide and ignore what's going on. I doubt I'd be welcomed back, anyway. It was less safe for them when I was there."

"I hope we both feel safe again someday."

He squeezed my hand. "Me too."

Chapter Thirty-Six

Peony had four bracelets ready for us that evening.

"Only four?" Alaric asked. "We need more than that."

"Stop complaining," Serena told him.

Peony smiled at her. "He's worried you'll leave him behind, and he won't be able to protect you. The foolish male doesn't appreciate your strength."

"Few do," Serena replied with a smile.

"This was all I could manage," Peony told us. "It takes a lot of energy, and I can't afford to drain myself to the point where I can't protect my people. If you come back in a week, I can have the others."

"We can't wait a week," I replied.

"Juliet is right," Dante agreed. "It's too risky for us to stay in this area another week. The bracelets will allow me, Juliet, Serena, and Sin to enter the Heathergate Refuge."

"I don't need a bracelet," Sin announced. "That spell isn't designed to keep demons out."

"It might have been nice to know this sooner," I complained. "You could have gotten word to my father."

"I'm not a messenger," Sin snapped. "Besides, they wouldn't likely have given me a chance to talk. People don't usually welcome help from demons."

"You're right," I replied. "Sorry for being so rude." My

attention shifted to Peony. "Thank you for all you've done."

She nodded. "You can stay another night and set out in the morning."

She walked away without waiting for a response.

"I'll take the fourth bracelet," Geori offered. "I'm the best fighter among us."

"Second best," Alaric corrected him.

Geori waved off his words. "Fine, second best, but you can't go with us. You're too high ranking among our people. You and the others should head back."

"I am your alpha," Alaric told Geori through gritted teeth. "I decide who accompanies Serena, and you aren't going."

"Why shouldn't it be Geori if he's your second best fighter?" I asked. "No one else in your group is likely to volunteer."

Alaric glared at me. "Since when do you even like Geori?"

I shrugged. "I don't hate him, but I wouldn't exactly say I like him. That isn't a requirement for him coming with us. Why are you arguing against this so hard?"

Alaric didn't want to let Serena go without him. That seemed like an even stronger argument for leaving him behind.

Alaric wasn't thinking clearly. He was acting volatile, like a male shapeshifter who'd recently found his mate. At the Heathergate Refuge, males were put on light duty when they first met their mate because they were so hard to deal with.

Since there was no magical bond between Alaric and Serena, I suspected his temperament would level out once they were apart. He usually seemed calmer when she wasn't nearby, so distance could be just what he needed. The only other option was claiming her as his mate, and he'd made it clear that would never happen.

"If anyone should go, it's me," Alaric bit out. "I'm better in a fight."

"Which is why you should stay with the rest of your

people," Dante told him.

"Exactly," I agreed. "You're their leader and responsible for their safety."

"It's time to let me go, Alaric," Serena whispered.

Alaric snorted. "This isn't about you, Serena. We've already discussed how any relationship between us is impossible."

"Yes, *you* have." This time, there was a note of sadness in her voice, as well as a finality. "It's time for you to go home. We appreciate all you've done for us, but this isn't your fight."

"You know I'm the right choice to go with them," Geori argued. "I'm expendable where you aren't. Besides, none of us want to return and be forced to explain your absence."

Alaric still didn't look happy, and he was glaring at his friend as he replied. "I don't know if you're lying to me or if you're blind to your real reasons for going with them."

"Knock it off, Alaric," Serena warned. "I am not in the mood to put up with your stupid games. Geori is my friend. Even if he has an ulterior motive, I trust him, and I like him."

Alaric looked down at his feet, clenching and unclenching his fists before letting out a tired sigh and nodding. "You're right. I'll let the others know."

He stormed off, barking out orders at the other shapeshifters.

"That was intense," Sin remarked with an eager smile. "I'm so glad she made four bracelets instead of three."

Dante rolled his eyes and muttered something about demons and drama.

"Are we leaving now?" Geori asked.

"No, I think we should wait until morning," I replied. "Tonight, we can make our final plans and get a good night's sleep."

"You should put that bracelet on before Alaric changes his mind," Serena suggested as she gestured to Geori's wrist.

"Why?" Geori asked. "He could still order me to take it

off and give it to him."

I shook my head. "It's not that simple. If you take it off, the bracelet is ruined."

"Good to know," Geori responded as he snapped the bracelet around his wrist. "Well, I'm committed now."

I put my bracelet on and said, "Hopefully, you don't regret that by this time tomorrow."

Chapter Thirty-Seven

I'd worn a bracelet my entire life, up until my stepmother had taken it from me, and it had always felt like a part of me. I hadn't noticed the soft hum of magic in those many years, but I noticed it now. After a few hours, I got used to the sensation, but the others still seemed bothered by it.

"I hate this bracelet," Geori muttered as he scratched around it.

"Stop messing with it," Serena told him with a frown. "You'll irritate your skin."

"Or break it," Dante added.

"They're fairly durable, but I wouldn't want to test its strength when we can't get a replacement," I stated.

Geori studied his bracelet. "They look delicate. I'm still surprised they adjusted perfectly to the size of all of our wrists. How do you keep them on your entire life? I'm not sure I could wear this thing for long."

I shrugged. "They're put on shortly after birth, so we're used to them."

The bracelet's spell allowed it to grow with us, so there was never a need to change one unless it got broken. I'd only heard of that happening twice.

"You'll get used to the magic," Serena assured him.

"I'm already finding it easier to wear. It's a lot more comfortable than that ankle cuff I had when I was under house arrest."

"Let's stop talking about the bracelets," Dante suggested as he pulled his sleeve down over his. "We're close to a trading post, so it would be best if we head off the trail and make our way east for a short time to avoid any Azureans."

"Or enemy shapeshifters," Serena added.

I nodded. "It's best if we don't run into anyone until we get past the Ivorfalls. I'd prefer to find my father first. He's the only one I know we can trust."

Dante squeezed my hand before releasing it. "We'll be there soon."

"I wish we had more shapeshifters with us." Geori suddenly froze.

"Someone's coming," I whispered.

We all hurried off the trail and crouched in the bushes.

I remained perfectly still as I listened to the group approaching on the trail. They were talking loudly, clearly not afraid of being overheard.

"This is a waste of time, Kaine," a male complained.

"Do you have something better to do with your day?" the male who had to be Kaine demanded.

"Anything is better than wandering around in this cold weather," the first male replied.

A female laughed. "Cold? You're too weak to be a Shadow Walker, Paulo. It's a perfectly nice day. Besides, if Kaine hadn't pulled you from rotation, you'd be on the peninsula where the wind is much colder."

I looked over at Dante, and he seemed just as surprised by the presence of the Shadow Walkers. This wasn't their hunting territory, and I'd never heard of them venturing so close to the Heathergate Refuge.

"Are we really going to use that excuse about getting tapaberry salve from the Azurean trading post?" Paulo asked.

"That's what I told the others we were doing, and they

bought it," Kaine replied. "Could you stop complaining? We'll be back home soon. I swear, I'm never taking you with me again."

"I was hoping for a good fight," Paulo complained. "Isn't that why you're here, Calista?"

"Nope," Calista replied. "I came because I need tapaberry salve. Kaine's excuse worked out well for me. Now, let's finish this wild goose chase and grab the salve. I have three patients who need it, and I'm running low."

"All right, Cal," Kaine replied. "We should be able to head back soon."

We waited several minutes to allow them to put more distance between us before stepping out of the bushes.

"Why are there Shadow Walkers this far out?" Serena asked with a frown.

Dante shrugged. "That's an excellent question. Tulurean healers travel to these trading posts for supplies, but we rarely see any Shadow Walkers out this way."

"They said something about a possible fight," Geori remarked. "Do you think they might be planning to attack the trading post?"

"Not likely," Dante replied. "Azureans and Tulureans may not spend much time together, but we aren't at war. I can't see any reason a Shadow Walker would attack a trading post."

"Regardless of why they're out here, I'd like to avoid them," I replied. "They're probably not happy about me impersonating a Shadow Walker."

"Yes, we should stay far from the Shadow Walkers," Serena replied.

Dante gestured to a break in the trees on the other side of the trail. "This will take us around the main trail and let out near the Ivorfalls if I read the map right."

I shook my head. "Actually, I think we need to go this way." I pointed behind us, not surprised when the others frowned. The brush was thicker, and it would be harder to pass through.

"The route you're suggesting is too well-maintained," I

explained. "Someone is using it, and we don't know if that person is an enemy. I think we should avoid that path."

"She makes a good point," Sin agreed. "I think we should take the less-traveled trail."

"All right," Dante agreed. "Do the two of you want to change into animal form."

"No," Geori replied without hesitation. "Let's get moving."

"All right," I reluctantly agreed, not sure staying in human form was safest. "It might be a good idea if we take out the hoodies we got from Peony."

Geori looked uneasy. "I don't know."

"I'm not sure I trust the spell she put on those," Dante added.

"They're fine," Sin argued. "All they do is help hide your identity when you have the hood up."

Serena nodded. "She's right, Dante. We examined the spell and didn't find anything unusual."

"How much do spellcasters know about demon magic?" Geori asked as he pulled the hoody from his pack and eyed it as if it might bite him.

Sin glared at him. "I know a lot about demon spells. Are you calling me a liar?"

"He doesn't know you well enough to know if he can trust you," Dante reminded her.

Sin's attention shifted to Dante. "Do you trust me?"

Dante nodded. "I do, and if you say the spell is safe, then I'll put on the hoody."

"Then let's go!" Sin changed to a large black dog and trotted ahead of us.

"How long until we get there?" Serena asked as we all put on our hoodies and followed Sin.

"An hour at most," I replied as a feeling of foreboding washed over me.

"Are you okay?" Dante asked with a hand on my shoulder.

I nodded. "Yes, I suddenly had the strangest sense of dread. It must be my nerves."

"I don't blame you for being nervous," Serena told me with a slight smile. "Let's hurry. The sooner you pass through the Ivorfalls, the sooner you can breathe a sigh of relief. It will be nice to have fewer enemies to look out for."

"Yes," I agreed. "Then, we'll only have to worry about the traitors among my people."

Chapter Thirty-Eight

We headed to the far east end of the Ivorfalls since we were less likely to run into anyone while crossing through to the Heathergate Refuge. There were no roads safe for vehicles, and the hunting wasn't as good in that area. It was also much farther from any trading posts.

Our plan was solid, and we had a good chance of making it to my father without anyone stopping us. I was almost home, and everything was going according to plan, yet my confidence was waning with each step. The closer we got, the more my sense of impending doom grew.

"I'm paranoid," I whispered to myself.

"No," Dante told me. "You're smart. It would be foolish to let your guard down."

"It's more than that," I argued as I pushed my hood back, feeling like I couldn't breathe with it on. "I feel like something bad is coming our way."

"I feel it too," Geori agreed as he pushed his hood back.

"It's probably just nerves," I said to try to reassure both of us before I heard a noise that made me freeze.

"What is it?" Dante asked.

"Someone is coming," Geori replied as he looked in the direction of those approaching.

They had to have been using some sort of cloaking spell to have gotten so close before any of us noticed their presence. There was no time to put our hoods back up before the small group of spellcasters stood only about ten feet away from us.

"Don't move!" one of the warlocks shouted.

I calmed my racing heart and faced them with all the confidence of a leader. There was no reason to worry since both Geori and I wore bracelets. We were protected.

"And who do you think you are to give me orders?" I demanded. "Do you know who I am? Do you think it's smart to attack the future ruler of the Heathergate Refuge?"

I raised my hand to make sure they saw my bracelet.

The spellcasters hesitated.

"Let us pass," I told them. "We have a truce with the Azureans, and you have no right to detain us."

They didn't move, and one shook his head. "According to the current leader, and we know his only heir is a young male. Now, who are you really?"

Once again, I pushed down my panic and reminded myself that the bracelet protected me. We needed to talk our way past the spellcasters. There were eight of them, so it was smart to avoid a fight.

Sin moved to Dante's side and let out a soft, rumbling growl.

"What is that?" one of the warlocks asked as he pointed at Sin.

"It's a dog," I replied. "You've seen them before, right? Or do you not have them in Azuredale?"

"That doesn't look like any dog I've ever seen," one said as he continued to eye the demon. "You need to come with us." He then gestured to Dante and Serena. "You two! Pull back your hoods."

"You have no authority over us," Geori told him. "The members of the Heathergate Refuge are protected. Let us pass so we can go home."

They hesitated again, and I began to feel some hope

that they'd let us go. I didn't recognize any of them, so they probably didn't know who I was.

Someone had placed guards around the Heathergate Refuge, and the only reason I could think of was that they were looking for us.

A familiar voice from the back of the group confirmed they were part of an ambush set for us.

"Let me through."

Nicolas stepped forward with an irritating smirk and an evil gleam in his silvery-blue eyes. He looked directly at Dante when he spoke again. "Push your hood back so we can all see your traitorous face."

What were the chances of us running into him or of him thinking of searching this close to the Heathergate Refuge?

I'd have said we had no chance of running into him if he weren't standing right in front of us, making me wonder if one of Peony's people, possibly even Erik, had betrayed us.

Going willingly with Nicolas wasn't an option. That meant we were in for a fight.

Both Dante and Serena pushed back their hoods and glared at Nicolas.

Nicolas seemed even more amused by Serena's presence. "If it isn't my sweet little cousin. I can't wait to spend some time alone with you when you're locked up."

He expected her to cower. It's what she'd always done in his presence, but Serena was no longer a frightened witch. I enjoyed seeing Nicholas's composure briefly slip when her lips curled into a smile.

"Your confidence is your weakness, Nicolas," she said in her sweetest voice. "You won't hurt me or my friends."

He laughed. "Such brave words."

"How did you find us?" Dante asked.

"Someone sent word to Azuredale after you procured those bracelets, so I knew you were heading this way. I also have guards posted in a couple of different areas," Nicolas replied. "There are even Tulureans looking for you." He turned to the other Azureans. "We'll deal with them when we get back to Azuredale." He looked directly at me. "Do you know what my reward is for capturing you?"

"No, and I don't care," I replied in a bored tone.

"You should." He sounded annoyed that I wasn't playing the game according to his rules. "I asked for one thing. I want you as my familiar. You're all mine."

"Over my dead body," Dante snarled.

Nicolas laughed. "Yes, little brother, that's the plan."

Out of the corner of my eye, I saw two shapeshifters emerge from behind the Ivorfalls spell. I couldn't make out who they were with the hazy mist of the spell still surrounding them.

With any luck, they were loyal to my father and would help even up the odds, though it was equally possible they were traitors loyal to my stepmother.

"Juliet?"

Relief washed over me when I recognized Fiona's voice. She'd been one of my father's most loyal guards for many years.

"Yes," I replied without taking my eyes off the Azureans. "I'm back."

"We all heard you were killed when you went to the trading post," Fiona said. "Your stepmother said she saw your body."

"Nidia said she saw rogue shapeshifters kill you," Darius, a younger guard of my father's, added.

"She lied," I told them. "She wanted me dead, but her plan failed."

"Enough!" Nicolas shouted. "I'm taking all four of these prisoners with me."

"You have no right to take any of our people," Darius snarled.

"That's right," Fiona agreed. "You can take the others, but Juliet is ours."

"She's right," one of the warlocks stated. "If the shapeshifter is from the Heathergate Refuge, we have no authority over her."

Nicolas's jaw clenched as he bit out his response. "Do not question my orders. We take them all and kill anyone who tries to stop us."

"You'll take no one!" I snapped. "Fiona and Darius, as your future leader, I order you to defend my companions. Without them, I *would* be dead."

Nicolas threw the first magical blast, and I barely dodged it. Even with the help of Fiona and Darius, we were outnumbered, and the spellcasters seemed determined to avoid getting close enough for us to fight, instead relying on magic.

We needed to get past the Ivorfalls.

Dante sent his magic pouring out, and it slammed into Nicolas, knocking him to the ground. I'd forgotten how much more powerful he was in my presence.

Unfortunately, I was at a disadvantage since there was no time to change forms.

Sin lunged and took one of the Azureans down before ripping out his throat while the rest of us couldn't get close enough to land a single blow.

"If you can take Nicolas down, we can make a run for it," I told Dante. "The others are only following his orders, so they may not pursue us."

Dante nodded, his focus remaining on his fight with his brother. The strain on their faces was obvious as they each tried to land a magical blow.

Nicolas must have decided he wouldn't be able to defeat Dante alone because he yelled, "Kill my brother!"

Three other warlocks joined him.

This gave the shapeshifters a chance to get closer to some of the spellcasters who were distracted with focusing on just one warlock. I landed a sidekick to one who was about to send a blast of magic at Dante.

"Look out, Serena!" Geori shouted.

I shouldn't have looked in her direction. Just as Sin knocked Serena out of the way of a magical blast, a warlock tackled me to the ground. My distraction gave the warlock an advantage.

His hands wrapped around my throat, and I clawed at his wrists as I gasped for air.

"Don't kill her!" Nicolas shouted from right beside us, having abandoned his fight with Dante.

When I looked over, I saw that Dante was struggling to remain on his feet as he blocked the magical attacks of the two warlocks.

"You aren't going to win." Nicolas sounded matter of fact rather than taunting. "I'll make you a deal."

"Screw you and your deals," I hissed as the warlock above me leaned close enough for me to slam the heel of my palm into his nose.

He howled in pain and released my throat, giving me time to shove him off and scramble to my feet.

Nicolas stopped the warlock as he was about to hit me with a magical attack. "Don't damage my familiar!"

"I will never be your familiar!"

Nicolas moved closer, blocking my kick with a laugh. "Is that so? Your side is losing, Juliet. I'll have you one way or another, but I'm willing to make you a very generous offer—one I strongly recommend you take."

"What are you offering?" I asked. I would not trust anything Nicolas offered, but I wanted to keep him distracted and hopefully find a way for us to escape.

"Surrender, and I'll let the others go," he replied.

I snorted. "Why should I trust you to let them go? We both know you want Dante dead."

"I do," he admitted. "I've dreamt of seeing my brother die a horribly painful death, but I'll let him go for you. You'll add a lot to my power just as you have to Dante's. You'd better decide quickly. Once your side loses, that offer is off the table."

"Why make the offer if you think my side is going to lose, anyway?" I asked.

Nicolas looked irritated. "I don't want to start a war with your people. Not only will you come with me, you'll tell everyone that you chose to bond with me as my familiar. You will tell everyone that you don't want to return to the Heathergate Refuge."

He was an idiot if he thought his plan would work. Fiona and Darius would be witnesses to the fact that I hadn't wanted to go with him. They'd never believe my change of heart. Nicolas would kill the others no matter what I did.

"And then you'll let everyone else go?" I asked.

Nicolas's expression turned even cockier. "Of course. You're the prize I want above all others."

"Won't the other Azureans insist on taking Dante and Serena with us?" I asked.

He shrugged. "They all work for me. I can't promise they won't be captured later. Both are still wanted criminals, but this will give them a chance to get away."

We wouldn't get a better opportunity. I nodded nervously. The nerves I didn't have to fake since there was no guarantee this would work. "Okay, I'll go with you."

I held out a hand, hoping he'd step toward me to take it.

Nicolas hesitated before stepping closer.

Once he was within striking distance, I spun and landed a kick to his chest that knocked the wind out of him as he fell back.

"Get to the Heathergate Refuge!" I shouted to the others as I started running.

Dante and Serena sent out larger magical attacks that pushed their opponents back before turning to flee. I suspected they'd used much of their remaining energy to give us more time to make a break for it.

"I'll kill them all while you watch!" Nicolas shouted from behind me.

Our feet pounded against the ground as we raced toward safety. We were nearly there when the Shadow Walkers we'd seen earlier blocked our path.

"No," I whispered.

In a panic, I tried kicking one of them.

"Dear goddess," one of the Shadow Walkers said softly. "It really is you."

I had no time to ask him about his strange words; red hot magic slammed into my back, stealing my breath just before everything went black.

Chapter Thirty-Nine

Dante

The magic swirling around us made it hard to see or hear anything. All I knew was that Juliet was in danger.

I had to get to her, but Sin wouldn't allow it. Having changed to human form, Sin shoved me hard enough to send me flying through the mist of magic.

When I hit the ground, the wind left my lungs, and I gasped for air.

Once I could breathe again, I raced toward the mist of magic surrounding the Heathergate Refuge, but it threw me back.

"Juliet!"

"What's happening?" Serena asked as she touched the magic guarding the area. Sparks shot out at her, and she jumped back.

The two shapeshifters from the Heathergate Refuge looked perplexed.

"I've never seen it do that before," the female remarked.

The male tried passing through, but the spell shoved him back, though not with as much force as when I'd tried to cross. He frowned. "It's locked us in here."

I tried reaching out to Juliet with my mind, but the magic preventing me from getting to her blocked our connection like at Reaper Ridge. I couldn't connect with her mind, so I had no way of knowing if she was hurt or even dead.

"This can't be happening," the female argued. "The spell only prevents others from entering this area. Everyone with a bracelet should be able to come and go with no problem." She glared at me and then Serena. "Spellcasters shouldn't be able to pass through."

"It's a long story," I began as I held up my arm to show them the bracelet. "These are special. I'll explain everything later, but for now, you need to know that we've been helping Juliet."

Their attention shifted to Geori. "I don't recognize you," the female remarked.

"I've also been helping Juliet."

"Yet, she's been captured, and we can't get to her," the female stated. "That seems more than a little suspicious."

I didn't plan to stand around arguing with them when I needed to find a way back to Juliet. She was alone and surrounded by enemies.

"Sin!" I shouted as I looked around, wondering where she'd gone. I didn't see her anywhere.

"I don't think she made it in here with us," Geori remarked.

"Who is Sin?" the male asked.

"Sin is the demon traveling with us," Serena replied as she studied the magical barrier. "Do you think she was the one who closed off the area?"

"Why would she do that?" the female asked.

"To protect me," I said with a sigh. "She's not nearly as concerned with saving anyone else."

"She saved me," Serena argued.

"I'm pretty sure she shoved me through the spell as well," Geori remarked.

"Someone also pushed me," the female added.

"Same here," the male told us.

"And she left Juliet out there with enemies," I grumbled.

The female shapeshifter studied me. "Why were you fighting with Juliet?"

"How did you get those?" the male added. "None of this makes any sense."

"You've already said that," I growled. "The woman I love—my other half—is trapped on the other side of this barrier with a bunch of spellcasters who want to harm her. My brother is with them, and he's a twisted bastard. I have to get to her."

"I know this is hard to believe, but Juliet is our friend," Serena told them. "She'd be dead, or worse if Dante hadn't rescued her from that trap her stepmother put her in."

"I failed her," I whispered.

"The demon is with her," Geori reminded me, but it gave me little comfort since Sin had saved everyone but Juliet.

"Don't assume the worst," Serena said as if reading my thoughts. "Sin may not have locked us in here."

"She's right," Geori agreed. "The demon may not have had a chance to get Juliet across before the barrier closed."

"I hope that's true, but I'm not counting on Sin to help Juliet. There has to be a way out of here," I said as I started walking away, sticking by the edge of the spell.

"Stop!" the female called out. "You need to come with us."

"No." I stopped and looked over my shoulder at her. "I'm going to walk the perimeter of this spell until I find a weak area, and then I'm going after Juliet."

"I'm going with you," Serena announced.

Geori looked torn. "Juliet risked her safety because she was afraid for her father and her people. Perhaps we should update her father on what happened and then see if we can get some back-up to come with us. There were too many spellcasters for us to fight alone."

"You can go with the shapeshifters to update Juliet's father and get help if you want," I told him. "I'm finding a way out of here."

The female nodded. "Darius, go back and tell Shea and Marcus what's going on. Tell no one else."

"But our leader will want to know," Darius argued. "We have to tell him and the others, Fiona."

Fiona shook her head. "Not until we know who we can trust. Marcus will get word to our leader. This should be enough to bring him out of isolation. I'm going with you to help rescue Juliet."

"Let's go," I said as I started walking along the edge. "First, I'm going to find Juliet, and then I'm going to make sure my brother can never hurt her again."

"No," Serena argued. "You can't kill Nicolas. It will haunt you."

"He has to die," I insisted.

She nodded. "Yes, and that's why I'm going to kill him. I should have done it the day we escaped with Juliet. I need to be the one to do this."

"All right," I agreed. "There has to be a break in this spell. I can't lose Juliet."

"That Shadow Walker recognized her," Serena stated.

"Shadow Walker?" Fiona asked.

"Yes," I replied. "The last three spellcasters to arrive were Shadow Walkers. Why do you sound like that's a bigger problem?"

"It could be a very big problem," she replied before turning to Darius. "Change of plans. Find our leader and tell him the sins of the Shadow Walkers have come back to haunt us."

"What exactly does that mean?" Darius asked.

"He'll know," she assured him. "We need to get to Juliet quickly."

"Why would the Shadow Walkers want to hurt her?" I demanded after Darius ran off.

"I don't know that they do," she admitted. "All I know is that they tried killing her mother the first time she changed forms."

"Her mother?" I asked.

She nodded. "Yes, Eliza Shadow Walker."

Juliet really was a Shadow Walker?

"If they hurt her, I'll kill every last one of them," I snarled.

Author's Note

Were you surprised by Juliet's origins? I was when the idea came to me. When I first started writing this series, I planned to include a distant spellcaster connection, but I never intended to have Juliet come face-to-face with the reality of her spellcaster heritage. As I become more curious about the Shadow Walkers and how they related to this new world, I knew they needed to be a bigger part of this series.

Check out Sins of the Shadow Walkers to find out what happens next in Dante and Juliet's story. That will be the final book in this story arc, but there will be more in this new world.

Authors and readers rely on reviews, so please take a moment to review this book.

About the Author

Born and raised in the San Francisco Bay Area, C.L. Bright is a hard-working homeschooling mom who loves music, cooking, and reading. Even with her busy schedule, she still manages to find time to explore her artistic side by writing tales of unique worlds.

A few middle school typing classes sparked her obsession with writing and launched her creative adventures. Since then, she has devoted herself to exploring the art of storytelling. For several years, she used a pseudonym to write adult romantic novels. When her writing piqued the interests of her daughters, she decided to venture into the young adult genre so they can also enjoy her books.

Ingram Content Group UK Ltd.
Milton Keynes UK
UKHW022245220623
423898UK00014B/1629